Row 22
Seats A&B

FREDERICK WATERMAN

─ ◆ ─

To Seanababe's Auntie —
Merry Christmas

Frederick Waterman

CANFIELD & MACKENZIE, PUBLISHERS
BOSTON

Published in the United States by Canfield & Mackenzie, Publishers, Boston.

ISBN: 0-972-67700-3

07 06 05 04 03   7 6 5 4 3 2
First Edition
Second Printing - July 2003
Library of Congress Control Number: 2002117148

The stories *A Schedule to Keep, The Return of Raspel, Photographs and Memories,
The Bargain, Musical Chairs, Trust Me, Brother and Sister, The Sketchbook, Last Flight From
Moscow, Here Tomorrow, A Promise to Eddie Gray, Not An Option, Three Stories, My Father's Gift,*
and *Picture Perfect* all previously appeared in *Hemispheres* magazine,
a Pace Communications publication.

Book design by Sheila Young Tomkowiak
Cover artwork by Peter Cooper

Printed in the United States of America on acid-free paper.

THE STORIES

———◆•◆•◆———

"Anything you can do, or dream you can, begin it. Boldness has genius, power, and magic in it."

— *Goethe*

A
Schedule
to Keep

The flight from London to New York was 160 miles from Heathrow when it leveled off at its cruising altitude of 34,000 feet.

In Row 22, Seat B, a tanned, young man in his early 20s, wearing blue jeans and a clean but wrinkled white button-down shirt, leaned forward and withdrew a thin, leather-bound book from the knapsack at his feet. Straightening up, he opened the book to the middle, spread it wide, and shook it slightly, causing a slender pen to slip out of the spine, followed by a photo that had been tucked between the pages.

He picked up the photo and regarded it for several minutes, then pulled down the tray in front of him and carefully placed the picture along the right side. Reopening the book, he flipped through its pages until he reached the back where, on the first blank page, he wrote the day's date and, beneath it, "Somewhere Over the Atlantic." On the next line, he began writing in the small, firm script that had already filled the journal's first 120 pages.

In Row 22, Seat A, Brian Allbeck sighed and closed the paperback book he'd bought from the news agent at the airport. In the first 34 pages, the suspense thriller had offered one detailed sex scene, two gruesome murders, and absolute proof that its plot was stolen from another book. Only Shakespeare could get away with doing that, Allbeck thought, depositing the paperback into the seat pocket before him.

Six-foot-two, lean and fit, Allbeck had turned 60 the week before, an occasion that his wife insisted upon celebrating with "a small soirée," as she termed it, which meant 200 people at a catered cocktail party he could not avoid. Possessed of the talent but not the taste for society, Allbeck was handsome in a weathered, craggy way that implied he knew a rougher side of life, an impression that contributed to his dominating presence and, he knew, helped immeasurably in business. His full head of white hair, combed straight back, added to his leonine looks and contrasted sharply with the well-tailored, blue pinstripe suit.

Allbeck was aware that he looked rather grand for coach class, but this morning's "quick meeting" with his team of solicitors had turned into a three-hour strategy session after the firm's latest takeover target, a family-controlled French textile business, announced its plan to fight him in the courts. By the time Allbeck arrived at Heathrow, his scheduled flight had departed. The only available seat on the next New York-bound airliner was 22A, and he was glad to have it.

As Allbeck glanced out the oval window next to him, his right hand spun the wedding band on his left ring finger. The stunning vista of white clouds and blue sky held no appeal, because in the past 10 days, he'd done enough high-altitude sightseeing on flights to Munich, Milan, and Barcelona. Resigning himself to a sooner-than-expected start on the files in his briefcase, he turned to his seatmate to gain access to the overhead storage bin when the photo on the tray caught his eye.

The picture showed an extraordinarily beautiful woman looking over her shoulder at the camera. She had reddish-brown hair and large brown eyes that possessed both an uncomplicated friendliness and a welcoming sexuality. Trying not to be obvious, Allbeck craned his neck slightly to get a better angle.

Without looking directly at the young man, Allbeck noted the clean-shaven face and combed, sun-bleached hair. An upper-class American, he was sure, and judging from the speed and intensity of the writing, one of the high-energy, highly organized, very ambitious types — a description, Allbeck realized, that would have fit himself perfectly at the same age.

Bored enough to be uncharacteristically intrusive, he cleared his throat and said, "She is a very pretty woman."

7

The young man looked up with the quick, easy smile that is so distinctively American. Then he followed the older man's eyes to the photo. "She is beautiful, isn't she? And she's even better-looking than that. I'm a lousy photographer."

"If you don't mind my asking, how old is she?"

"Twenty-one."

"A model?"

"No," the young man grinned, "and she won't be unless the fashion world moves from Paris and New York to the Yorkshire Dales. She's a Yorkshire girl who's never been to London and hasn't any interest in going there either."

"You're joking," Allbeck replied.

"It's absolutely true. Two men who've known her all her life vouched for it."

"I take it that you just met her?"

"Right, eight days ago."

"And I hope that you spent every day since then with her."

"No, actually, I didn't. I had a schedule to keep."

"A schedule! What are you, mad?" Allbeck said in mock dismay. "What in blazes were you doing that was so important?"

"Bicycling from London to Edinburgh. It's something I've always wanted to do. It's on my list."

"Your list?" Allbeck repeated, the humor draining from his voice.

The young man flipped to the front of the journal. Inside the cover, below the name Thomas Landers, was a neatly typed list. He handed the journal to the older man.

Allbeck read the 11 lines to himself: *1. Win Rhodes Scholarship to Oxford. 2. Graduate in top three from law school. 3. Clerk for Supreme Court Justice. 4. Own a new Mercedes-Benz. 5. Run own law firm by the age of 37. 6. Take the Trans-Siberian Express across Russia. 7. Be a judge by the age of 50. 8. Bicycle through England and Scotland. 9. Understand Einstein's Theory of Relativity. 10. Learn to fly a plane. 11. Own a Picasso.*

He read through it twice in silence, his face revealing nothing, then handed the journal back. Thomas Landers' attempt at restraint gave way to curiosity. "What do you think?"

Allbeck sidestepped the query. "The red check marks — are they what I assume?"

"Yep. Three down, eight to go. I won the Rhodes Scholarship two years ago and learned Einstein's Theory of Relativity last year. This spring, I got my degree from Oxford in Politics, Philosophy, and Economics, and two weeks later started the bicycle trip." Landers' confidence was losing some of its bounce. The absence of the expected admiration was unsettling.

"How old were you when you drew up the list?" Allbeck's voice was subdued.

"Eighteen. You've got to set goals and these are mine."

Landers tapped a finger against the list. "This is my future."

Allbeck nodded thoughtfully. "Tell me about the girl. What's her name?"

"Cinda." The conversation's abrupt change caught Landers by surprise.

"And how did you meet her?"

"Well, you know it's been a cold, rainy summer in England and that slowed me down a lot, especially going through the Cotswolds. Bicycling in the rain is just plain stupid, you understand," Landers said, wondering why he felt a need to explain. "You never get far, you always get sick, and cars can't see you. Anyway, I finally reached Yorkshire just as another downpour began. I stayed dry under an oak tree, but the rain never let up. For the next five hours, the wind kept getting colder and colder.

"At about six o'clock, the rain finally stopped, but I didn't even make another mile before it started again. I was passing through this village, and there was a small pub, so I put my bike behind it and ducked inside. It was like I'd stepped into another century. Inside that pub, it could have been the 1890s or the 1790s. The ceiling was low with thick beams, and the walls were all made of wood that wasn't cut by any modern machinery. Most of the light came from the fire in this great, stone fireplace.

"About 20 men were there, and most of them looked like farmers. When I walked in, they all turned and looked at me as if I'd just barged into their house, not their pub. It felt like a scene out of a Western where the stranger comes into town and everyone just watches him. Anyway, I sat down next to the fire to get warm, and this beautiful woman appeared. She asked what I wanted to drink, but when she saw I was shivering, she brought me a hot buttered rum. 'We don't make a lot of these in the summer, but I think I still remember how,' she said, then pulled up a chair in front of me and made sure that I drank it all.

"When I got warm enough to put together coherent sentences, we started talking. She said that her name was Cinda and that her father owned the pub, just like his father had, his grandfather, and his great-grandfather, but Cinda's father was off that night. She asked me what an American was doing in Yorkshire in the rain, and I explained that I was on my way from London to Edinburgh. That's when she said she'd never been to either city or even gone more than 100 miles from Yorkshire. Despite that, as she spoke, you could tell she was smart. And when we talked about the English countryside, she was the one who could quote Tennyson, Wordsworth, and Keats.

"While we were talking, I didn't have to look around to know that the men at the bar were keeping their eyes on us, as if they were all Cinda's uncles. It felt like I was on a date with 20 chaperons.

"Cinda got up occasionally to serve the men, but we weren't interrupted too often because, as she put it, 'They're here for the talking more than the drinking.' The evening passed and, well, you never know what people see in you, but at about 10 o'clock, one of the men brought a pint of beer over to me and, eventually, all of us were sitting in front of the fire. When they left, each of them shook my hand and the last one, the biggest one, said in a real low voice, 'Good night, young fella. You be careful with our Cinda.' And there was no doubt that he meant it.

"When she began cleaning up, I helped because I didn't know if I was expected to leave too — though I didn't want to. Afterward, Cinda put two thick logs on the fire and poured a full glass of brandy for me. Do you know those conversations you can have with only a very few people? Those times when every word's understood just the way you meant it, and you never have to explain anything? That's what this was like. I told her about the places I'd been, and she told me about the people in her town, and we told each other what we wanted in our lives.

"We talked all night, and the funny thing is that I never got tired. Somehow, talking with her was restoring, almost restful. When it started to get light outside, she asked me what was the best dawn I'd ever seen. When I started to tell her about one, she just shook her head. 'The best dawn you've ever seen is the one you're about to see,' she said.

"The rain had stopped during the night, the clouds had cleared out, and there was a perfectly blue sky. She took my hand, and we walked up a hill that seemed to go straight up until, from the top, you could see the whole valley, which

opener under the flap, and carefully ripped through the adhesive tape. With two fingers, he withdrew the yellowed piece of paper.

Allbeck took a deep breath and opened the page. His eyes swept down the column of black X's and, for a moment, dread overcame him, then he saw the firm red check mark and "June 29, 1997, Yorkshire, England" on the ninth line, the line he hadn't been able to cross off himself, the line that read "Marry for Love." ♦

The Return of Raspel

"Raspel, his back pressed against the wall of the Paris hotel's dim hallway, screwed the silencer onto the .38 caliber automatic. From inside Room 51, he could hear the low voices of the Moroccan diplomat and his Russian spyhandler. Raspel's first shot would be through the Moroccan's heart — that was the kill he'd been hired for — it was the second shot, at Kaborasov, that Raspel had anticipated for five years. Ever since Berlin. And before Kaborasov died, he would hear two words: "Monique Tristan," and he would realize who was about to kill him — and why. Raspel eased off the safety and kicked open the door to Room 51."

L ouis Gates, sitting in Row 22, Seat A, put down his pen and reread what he'd written. Should somebody else be in the room, he wondered, someone who hadn't spoken? That would make it tougher on Raspel. He would still shoot the Moroccan first, maybe need two shots to finish the unexpected third person, and, by then, Kaborasov would have his gun out. Gates couldn't make it too easy for Raspel.

Suspense and danger were the foundation of espionage novels, but, of course, he wouldn't kill off his lucrative legend in *The Return of Raspel*. A four-book contract for $20 million guaranteed that.

Outside the window next to Gates, there was nothing to see. It was night, and the cloud cover was so thick he didn't even try to look for lights below. Instead, he glanced at his watch. The time was 8:15 p.m. GMT, which meant the airliner must still be over the Continent; the English Channel was at least another 10 minutes away.

As usual, Gates was traveling alone, though as a former foreign correspondent, he was used to it. What he wasn't used to anymore was traveling in coach, but first class was sold out.

In his mid-50s, Gates was just under medium height with thinning gray hair and humorless eyes. The face that had appeared on the back of several million books could have been handsome in a stern way but for his mouth's natural expression of peevish irritability. Gates' clothes were expensive, especially the Italian silk sportcoat tailored to hide his paunch. Five best-sellers allowed him to indulge his vanity.

In the late 1980s, Gates was working as the European correspondent for a Chicago newspaper when he wrote his first book. Nine publishing houses turned it down. At the tenth, an editor bluntly told him that he wasn't much of a writer and that he lacked imagination. But she said that in the morass of his words, there was one memorable minor character.

"I don't know how it happened in your book, Mr. Gates, but this Raspel is intriguing. He makes his living killing people, and yet the reader somehow ends up rooting for him. I wanted to know what he was thinking and why, where he'd been and where he was going. Except for him, your book's about as interesting as a doorstop."

Ten months later, Gates had completed a new thriller, this time using Raspel as the central character. The day he signed the book contract, he quit his job; six months later, the movie offer made him a millionaire.

In each of Gates' best-sellers, Raspel was the hero/villain, an assassin whose self-devised code of ethics set him apart from the world he operated in. Raspel became so popular that the roguish French actor cast in the role needed only two films to jump from anonymity to worldwide fame.

And yet, despite Gates' own success, he knew that the

publishing-house editor was right: He was basically a lousy fiction writer who had stumbled upon a great character, though his ego prevented him from admitting this to anyone. A second truth was common knowledge — that Raspel wasn't Gates' creation. In the late 1970s, there had been a legendary assassin-for-hire from Israel, an elusive lone operator named Raspel who was ingenious in his methods, earned half a million dollars per kill, and reportedly turned down any job if he admired the target.

Then, after seven years, Raspel disappeared. The ruler of a small, oil-rich country in the Middle East, believing that he was Raspel's next target, had placed a $4 million bounty on the assassin's head. Although the bounty was never publicly claimed, the ruler ceased to fear for his life, and nothing more was heard of Raspel.

Fifteen years later, the myth, polished and embellished by Gates, had spread around the world. So few facts were known about the true Raspel — including his real name — that the best-selling version had to be invented. Gates decided that Raspel was fluent in half a dozen languages, that he had been trained by the Mossad and in the Orient, and that he could change his appearance to suit an opera house or an alley. And even though Raspel was a man of no distinctive characteristics, he did possess one remarkable trait — an intense life force, an almost tantalizing energy that women were keenly aware of.

Gates picked up his pen again. He could grind out a few

more paragraphs before the jet reached Heathrow. Then he'd have a 35-minute taxi ride to his house in Belgrave Square, where he'd drop off his bags before continuing on to Claridge's for a late dinner. What was his date's name? Oh, yes, Alissa. Beautiful and not too bright. That's the way he liked them.

"Pardon me," said a voice close by. Gates looked up at the man sitting next to him, who had been asleep since takeoff. "Aren't you Louis Gates?"

The author sighed. The thrill of autographs had worn off long ago. To Gates, fame was only good if the person who recognized him was an attractive woman.

"Yes, I am," he replied, his mouth twisting into something closer to a grimace than a smile.

"I've read all your books," said the man, who appeared to be in his mid- to late 40s, had a full head of black hair, and dark, very intense eyes.

Gates offered the usual words of thanks as he noted his seatmate's herringbone jacket, open shirt, and nearly black trousers, but he was stumped by the man's nationality. The facial features were strong, almost Egyptian, and yet there was something of the aristocratic Spaniard in him, or was it Turkish? The man's words provided no clue, for they were almost untainted by accent. Oh, who cares, Gates thought, looking back down at the page before him.

The man in Seat B wouldn't take the hint.

"In fact, I've read each book two or three times," he continued. His tone had changed; it lacked any hint of flattery. Gates looked up, uncertain.

"I guess I'm like all your other readers," the man said. "The character of Raspel is what interests me. He's not like the assassins or spies in other espionage novels. There's so much more to him."

Gates relaxed. His seatmate was headed toward the familiar "Golly, you're wonderful" idolatry. Gates had heard it a thousand times and the praise bored him.

"I know that you patterned Raspel after someone." The seatmate was speaking softly, thoughtfully, almost as if he were talking to a child. "I read that he was killed for that bounty." The man turned and looked directly at Gates. From 18 inches away, the stare was unnervingly close. "But what if he wasn't?"

A wave of uneasiness swept through Gates. "Pardon me?" he asked, hoping that he'd misunderstood.

"What if he wasn't killed?" The voice was frighteningly gentle. "What if Raspel were still alive?"

Gates' mouth went dry. Transfixed, he looked into the dark, depthless eyes before him, where no human connection registered. Gates tried to calm himself but his mind began whirling. Was Raspel dead? Of course! He'd died 15 years ago! Gates had been writing fiction about a dead man, making up Raspel's every word, thought, and action. If Raspel were alive, he'd be in his mid- to late 40s and ... Gates shrank back. The high seat backs before and behind him felt like walls, penning him in. The stranger blocked him from the aisle. And if Gates reached the aisle, where would he go at 25,000 feet?

The man in Seat B waited, patient and composed, as if he'd waited a long time to hear Gates' answer. The author struggled for self-control. Twice, he opened his mouth, but no words came out.

"I'll tell you what I think," the stranger said evenly. "I think that if Raspel were alive, he'd come and get a look at you, at the man who made him so famous. That seems quite logical, doesn't it?"

Gates gave a slow, almost obedient nod.

"After all, if someone were writing about you, describing how you felt and what you thought and what you believed in, wouldn't you wonder where he got his ideas? It's rather like someone painting your portrait without ever setting eyes on you, isn't it? So, tell me how you developed Raspel."

"I ..." Gates faltered, "I knew a few people at Interpol and the French Surete. They had files on Raspel but there were no pictures or interviews. No hard facts, only rumors. The CIA didn't know any more about him either."

The dark eyes waited.

"There were stories," Gates continued uncertainly, "that Raspel lost his family when he was young. I heard that his father was a soldier and his mother a linguist. I also heard it the other way around — that she was one of the highest-ranking women in the Israeli military. Nobody's sure who Raspel really was. He was highly intelligent and left nothing to chance, that's certain. The only way to recognize his kills was the lack of any clues. That was his only pattern ..."

"But what about his soul?" the stranger interrupted. "You made him a saint and a sinner! Or do you think he's just a madman?"

Here was the core of Raspel, and the man in Seat B wanted to hear it. Gates had never told anyone how, in the only inspired moment of his life, he'd attached an old memory to the legend of Raspel. Now he was too unnerved not to tell the truth.

"Thirty years ago, in Texas, I covered the execution of a man who'd killed six people. Just before the hood was put over his head, the priest gave him last rites. I never forgot it because the priest was his brother, his twin. They looked so alike, I wondered how different they really were under the same shared skin. I think of them when I write about Raspel."

"Did you ever meet anyone who knew the real Raspel?"

"Twenty or 30 claimed to," Gates answered, "but, after a while, they'd get their stories mixed up. They couldn't keep the dates and places straight. Some of them talked about Raspel as if he were a great hero; some talked about him as if he were a villain."

"And what do you think? Is Raspel a hero, a mercenary, or a psychopath?"

Gates wished that he had the nerve to challenge the stranger and demand, "What difference does it make to you?" Instead, he looked down, and he could only manage a small shrug.

"I see," said the man in Seat B, his voice absolutely flat. "Now, Mr. Gates, I'm going to tell you what happened to Raspel, and I want you to pay attention. After seven years of killing, Raspel found out that fear can be more useful than death. Shoot one dictator and his replacement is drinking brandy in the palace by nightfall. They replace each other like weeds in a garden.

"But if you show a dictator how easily you could kill him, he will bargain. When his car explodes a moment after he leaves it, or his dinner makes him ill but does not poison him, he will bargain. Then he will agree not to execute a dissident or an opposition leader, or will decide to release more medicine to his people. And he might even agree to lift a $4 million bounty he's placed on another man's head. Fear, you see, is a remarkable thing."

The hum of the jet engines changed slightly and Gates sensed the plane's descent. Fifteen minutes to Heathrow. The stranger would have to let him out.

"Let me make a suggestion," said the man in Seat B. "Forget about Raspel being any kind of psychopath. He always knew what he was doing, but sometimes we are forced to do things we don't want to do. And we do things that others don't understand. I'm sure you'd agree with me, Mr. Gates."

25

It wasn't a question, but Gates nodded anyway.

"Good," said the stranger. "Raspel's existence is in your hands, and I hope that you will take great care of him." The stranger reached out a finger and lightly flipped the lapel of Gates' expensive jacket. "That is only fair, of course, for it seems that Raspel has taken very good care of you." And with that, the man in Seat B turned away from Gates and closed his eyes.

The best-selling author didn't remember breathing for the final 10 minutes of the flight, nor did he look directly at the motionless figure at the edge of his peripheral vision.

The stranger did not acknowledge Gates again. When the plane rolled to a stop, he stood up, slipped through the people filling the aisle, and was among the first to disembark.

It took Gates nearly 15 minutes to walk through Heathrow to the taxi stand. His heart rate was finally slowing, and he could almost breathe normally when he stepped through the airport's exit doors into the cool air. The rain beyond the overhang was hard and steady as it pelted the passing cars. On the far side of the wide ramp, Gates saw a wet, black Mercedes, its wipers throwing water off the windscreen, and the passenger door closing, allowing just a glimpse of the arm and shoulder of a herringbone jacket.

The Mercedes pulled away from the curb. Gates stepped forward, oblivious to the drenching rain. Peering at the car, he thought he could see a blond-haired woman behind the wheel. The man in the passenger seat turned, looked across at Gates, and his hand came up to the window, one finger pointing at the author as if it were a gun; then the Mercedes disappeared into the nighttime traffic. Gates stood in the rain, frightened, somewhat dazed, and very relieved.

"Who was that little man, darling?" Sarah Nassim asked her husband as she weaved the Mercedes around an old Volvo.

"That, my dear," said Roger Nassim in his British accent, "was Louis Gates."

"The author?" she exclaimed, visibly excited.

"Exactly. He sat next to me on the flight."

"How wonderful! Did you tell him how much you like his books?"

"I told him that I'd read them all twice."

"Oh, I wish I'd been there! Was he as entertaining as his stories? The two of you must have had an absolutely fascinating conversation!" she exclaimed. "But, you know, Roger, even if he does sell millions of books, I've heard the stories that you make up for the children, and you've got twice the imagination he does."

"Hmmm," was Roger's only reply. Sarah glanced over at him and saw the mischievous glint in his eyes.

"What have you gone and done?" she said, breaking into a smile as she cut into the next lane and accelerated. "Did you make up some story?" Sarah glanced again at her husband and saw his wide grin.

"Why, you did! He was standing in the rain looking frightfully worried! You've scared the willies out of him! Oh, Roger," her voice lilted playfully, "you are a wicked, wicked man!" ♦

Photographs and Memories

"Down in the mine, our yellow bird sang,
Her notes high and true all day,
And then one morn her pretty song stopped,
And we knew it was time to pray."

The Whisper Chorus was hard at work, thought Owen Llewellyn, listening with a smile. The nine burly Welshmen, trying not to bother the other passengers on the L.A.-Boston flight, were singing in whispers so soft that the coal miners' song sounded as if it were being sung by angels. The lads were always ready to break into song and, when the choir members next to him in Row 15 began, the ones in Rows 14 and 16 quickly leaned over the seat backs and joined in.

Fifteen concerts in a dozen U.S. cities over 18 days required a lot of flying, which was how the Whisper Chorus developed. Self-entertaining and almost inaudible from 12 feet away, the whispered songs helped shorten

29

every flight, and, as one of the younger men observed, "it attracts the ladies better than anything except a pup." Right now, a slender woman with short red hair was standing in the aisle next to Owen's seat, leaning in to hear the song while trying to stay out of the way of the flight attendants and other passengers.

Owen stood up and, telling the woman that he was going to stretch his legs for a while, offered his seat. She took it with a word of thanks, barely taking her eyes off Davy, the broad-shouldered tenor from Glyncorrwg who joined the 30-member Cardiff Men's Choir just four months ago.

Owen moved down the aisle, aware that half a life ago he had been one of the energetic lads complaining that the choir's annual U.S. tour was too short. Now he was in his mid-50s, and every trip seemed at least a week too long. Age wasn't the problem, it was simpler than that. The truth was that he missed his wife.

Every day at their jeweler's shop, it was "Mr. Llewellyn" and "Mrs. Llewellyn," their tone always formal, both in front of the staff and alone. Each evening, during the drive home, they held hands as they discussed the day's work. It is odd how you get used to the feel of someone, Owen thought as he slipped into an empty aisle seat in Row 22. Perhaps a few more U.S. tours and he'd tell the choirmaster that it was time to give his spot to someone else. He could invent a reason or perhaps just say that business was up at the shop — which was always true — and he couldn't afford to be away for so long.

Owen closed his eyes, hoping for sleep, but it wouldn't come. They'd boarded the plane at 9 a.m. Pacific Standard Time, and his internal clock was supplying him with middle-of-the-day energy and alertness.

"I'm going home," said a woman's voice to his left.

Owen opened his eyes and saw, across the aisle and next to the window, a woman in her 70s. Apparently, the man in Seat B had asked the usual traveler's question.

"Back to Snowdon, Vermont," she said, with a smile that made all the delicate lines in her face fall into place. Owen noticed that the woman was dressed with great style, her black suit was tailored and the double string of pearls served to emphasize the white purity of her hair. Here, he thought, was a woman who had been beautiful at every age.

"And what's it like in Snowdon, Vermont?" asked the man in Seat B, who was dressed in a rougher manner, wearing corduroy trousers, a flannel shirt, and scuffed outdoorsman's boots. He had a full head of gray hair, intelligent eyes, and seemed robustly healthy. Owen couldn't guess the man's age or background. The weathered complexion suggested someone who'd spent much of his life outdoors. Owen wondered what an American rancher would look like, or if there were even any left.

"Would you really like to hear about my town?" the woman asked.

"I really would," said the man in the seat next to her.

31

"Then I'll tell you." She drew a deep breath to begin, then stopped. "I'm sorry, my name is Abigail Clark."

"I'm Richard Kendall."

"It's nice to meet you, Richard. Snowdon is a little town of 4,000 people, and it hasn't changed much since the last century. In town hall, there's a map from 1869, and if you took it down and walked around using only that to find your way, you'd never get lost."

"It sounds as if you remember this place pretty well."

"I remember it perfectly!" she said proudly. "I can tell you which family lived in which house, who worked in which store, who were the town gossips and town drunks, and exactly which flowers my mother planted in our garden out back."

Richard Kendall was turned away from Owen, but the amusement in his voice made it easy to imagine his expression. "So, tell me, what was it like growing up in Snowdon, Vermont?"

"Well, during winter everyone called it 'Snowed-in,' and we usually were. The town's on the east side of Ethan's Lake and, until late December when the lake finally froze over, every winter storm would pick up moisture off that lake and give us an extra six inches of snow.

"And when the ice was thick enough, at each full moon — whether it was a weekend or school night — bonfires were built along the shore, and we all went skating. It was magic," she said and closed her eyes for a moment, savoring the memory.

"What did the town look like?" Richard asked.

"Most towns have a main street, but Snowdon's different. Everything's built around the town common, which is shaped like a triangle. Town hall, the library, the schools, the churches, the stores, and some of the oldest houses all face the common."

"And you lived in one of those houses?"

"I did, and it was the nicest house in town, three stories high, with white clapboard and black shutters. My great-grandfather built it in 1872, after his first house burned down. When I was born, I became the seventh generation of Clarks to live on that site."

Was anyone in her family still living there, Owen wanted to know, but he was outside the conversation, and Richard Kendall didn't ask the question.

"I was the seventh generation, and my father always said that I got into more trouble than the other six combined," Abigail said, laughing. Owen realized that she was gently flirting with the man next to her.

"Were you a tomboy?" Richard asked.

"Worse! I was a troublemaker! My mother claimed that if there were two doors in front of me, one labeled 'Safe and Easy' and the other 'Fun and Trouble,' I'd go for 'Fun and Trouble' every time."

"What sort of mischief did you get into?"

"Well, the worst was on the Fourth of July when I was

eight years old. I decided that the higher you could get, the better the fireworks would look. So, I convinced the boy next door that we should sneak into the Methodist Church and climb up to the bell tower.

"We went up there at sunset and crawled out onto the ledge, right next to the church bell. It was so high we were both scared to death, though neither of us would admit it. Anyway, we were right, that bell tower was the best place to see the fireworks! And, an hour later, when no one could find us, we had a perfect view of everyone running all over town looking for us. When they finally found us, we got in all kinds of trouble."

"But you're glad you did it, aren't you?" Richard said.

"I'd never been up so high. It seemed, from there, like we could see the whole world, and I remember thinking how small Snowdon looked! I realized then that the world was a lot bigger than I'd thought, and I promised myself I'd see as much of it as I could."

There was a slight pause in the conversation. Ask her what she saw, Owen silently urged Richard Kendall. Where did she go? How much did she see? Did she keep her promise to herself?

But the moment passed, and Abigail turned the conversation around. "And what kind of work do you do?"

"I'm a photographer," Richard replied.

"Really! What kind of pictures do you take?"

"Every kind. For the first 20 years, I was a nature photographer because I was like you, I wanted to travel, and the camera was my excuse. Then, after 68 countries, I'd made a reputation and was ready to settle down for a while. I did portrait work for a long time, including four years as the president's photographer."

"At the White House!" Abigail exclaimed.

"1600 Pennsylvania Avenue. I showed up at the South Gate at 8 o'clock every morning."

Abigail reached over and grabbed Richard's arm. "You're not moving until you tell me about what you've seen and done!"

"What if I show you some pictures instead?"

"Deal!" she exclaimed, letting go of his arm. Richard reached under the seat before him and, from a leather satchel, withdrew a stiff manila envelope. He put down the two tray tables in front of them, pulled out four photographs from the envelope and spread them across the trays. Across the aisle, Owen discreetly craned his neck, trying to see them all.

"Oh, my," said Abigail, looking at the picture directly in front of her. "That's no cuddly white bear; he looks like he's ready to kill you!"

The mostly white picture showed a polar bear at dangerously close range, pulling himself out of an ice-strewn sea onto a slab of ice. He was staring at the camera with hungry malevolence.

"That was inside the Arctic Circle, just off the top of

Norway," Richard explained. "The ice floe I was on had just split when he came up out of the water and decided that I would make a good dinner. I took this picture, then jumped over the gap to the other half of the floe before it got too far away. Oh, he was angry!"

Did the bear try to follow, Owen wanted to know, but Abigail didn't ask. She was already staring at the next photo, which must have been taken from a plane, Owen thought, for it looked down upon a range of snow-covered mountains. The photo's most striking feature was the blazing red sky, cut through with twisting streaks of yellow and black. The sky looked like a wave of fire about to sweep down on the white mountains and consume them.

"Taken from a balloon over Nepal," Richard said. "Sunrise — looking east toward Katmandu. 'Hell's Dawn' was the only title possible."

"I don't think I've ever seen mountains look defenseless," Abigail said in wonder. Her gaze slid over to the next picture, but she looked away almost immediately.

"The Everglades, Florida," Richard said.

The photograph showed a long-legged white bird, an egret, Owen guessed, standing on a tuft of marsh grass as if it were posing. To the right, a few feet away on the water's surface, were the wet, reptilian eyes of a submerged alligator. The egret and the alligator were looking at each other. What the bird didn't see was that, behind it, the jaws of another alligator were open and approaching.

"I don't like that picture," Abigail said.

"How about this one?" Richard replied and flipped up the photograph, revealing another. The jaws of the alligator on the left were blurred, moving too fast to be stopped by the camera's shutter speed, but along the top edge of the picture was a pair of webbed bird's feet.

"He escaped!" Abigail exclaimed.

"He did," Richard nodded. "I took the picture, then I popped a flash, scaring the bird."

"Good for you," she said, then looked at the final photo, the one in front of Richard. Owen already knew the picture, which had appeared in newspapers and magazines all over the world, and he remembered the story behind it. A hurricane hit the Carolinas, killing 70 people, and the president went to survey the damage. In the background of the black-and-white photo was the wreckage of a house and, in the foreground, the president was kneeling, listening to a little girl who couldn't find her friend. The president's face was wet with tears, and the girl had reached out her hand, touching his tears.

After a long moment, Abigail said, "It's beautiful."

"Sometimes you're in the right place," Richard said simply.

Owen expected another series of photos to be laid out, but instead Abigail yawned. "I'm sorry," she said, "I'm a little tired. I hope you don't mind, but I need a nap."

"Not at all," Richard said. "It was a pleasure talking to you."

Abigail closed her eyes and, in less than a minute, Owen heard the deep, rhythmic breathing of sleep. As Richard slid the pictures back into their envelope, Owen realized that the man seemed suddenly older. The energy so evident throughout the conversation was gone, replaced by a somber reverie.

"Your pictures are extraordinary," Owen ventured.

Richard looked up, surprised.

"I apologize for eavesdropping," Owen added.

"No problem," Richard said, managing only a distracted half-smile.

"I was hoping she would want to see more of your work."

"She tires quickly," Richard said. "You see, she's not at her best anymore."

Owen hesitated. "You know her?" he asked, confused.

"She's my wife," Richard said quietly.

"But your conversation ..."

"She doesn't know me — not for the past two years."

"But her memory was so good ... all those details about her growing up ..."

"That's how it happens sometimes," Richard said softly. "First she lost the present, then the recent past, then all of her adult life. It's eaten its way back through her life. She doesn't know that she ever became Abigail Kendall. She doesn't remember our marriage, our daughter, our son, where we went, or what we did." Richard gestured toward the envelope. "Abby was there when I took each of those pictures. She was the one who popped the flash and scared the bird away. I never went anywhere without her."

He looked at the woman next to him, then laced his fingers through hers, which tightened reflexively around her husband's. The mind could lose its memories, but habits were stored elsewhere, Owen thought.

Richard turned back. "At first, I tried to tell her about the places she'd been, but it only frustrated her as she realized how much she couldn't remember. Abby had wanted to see the whole world, and she did, and now she's lost it all, except that for a while every day, I can give her back a little bit. She can have the excitement of being in those places where the pictures were taken." Daily discovery instead of old memory, Owen thought.

"Are you really taking her to Vermont, to where she grew up?"

Richard nodded. "It's the only place she knows anymore. I've rented the house she grew up in. For a month or two, she'll know where she is. She won't be lost when she walks outside. The whole world won't be strange to her."

For several minutes, Owen Llewellyn and Richard Kendall sat in silence, their private thoughts unshared. Then Owen stood up, reached out, and shook the other man's hand. "Good luck," he said, then paused. "May I ask how long you've known her?"

"All my life," Richard replied. "You see, I was the boy next door."

Owen nodded and turned away. He walked up the aisle, looking left and right, searching for the choirmaster. It was time to tell him how good business had been at the shop. ♦

The Bargain

"You must be the worst cab driver in the world! Haven't you ever been to an airport?"

Anthony Cerruti looked into the rear-view mirror, at the blazing eyes of the woman behind him. When he'd picked her up outside the Amoco Building in downtown Chicago, she'd looked so beautiful, but her appeal hadn't survived the 80-minute, rush-hour crawl from the Loop to O'Hare International.

"Are you trying to make sure that I miss my flight?"

The fare glowed red on Anthony's meter: "$48.90." That's a fair price, he thought. In fact, it would be a bargain. He would gladly pay $48.90 to get her out of his cab.

"What are you waiting for, an invitation? Pull in here!"

Ahead, a white minivan loaded down with children and suitcases was moving away from the curb. Anthony, seeing that the van's lights remained off, flicked his headlights twice. The van's red taillights lit up in response, and the driver waved.

"Come on, Mr. Good Samaritan, hurry up!"

Anthony pulled into the open space and stopped the meter.

"Airport tax adds one dollar to the fare," he said.

The beautiful woman dropped three crumpled bills into the front seat. Two $20s and a $10. Anthony didn't thank her for the 10-cent tip. She stepped out of the cab, her briefcase in one hand, a garment bag and leather satchel in the other, then kicked the door shut with such force that everyone in the unloading area looked up.

Andrea Bain was not the kind of woman whom men just glanced at. Every male in front of Terminal 1 noticed the thick, auburn hair; the figure that could not be hidden by a business suit; and the long, slender legs. She strode into the airy, blue-and-white terminal, glanced at the departures screen, and relaxed. Her flight had been delayed 20 minutes.

Andrea passed between the busy ticket counters, turned left toward Concourse B, and saw that the line at the security gate was 15 deep. She never hesitated. Walking to the front, she announced, "My flight is leaving immediately!" and placed her briefcase and bags on the conveyor belt. She stepped through the metal detector before anyone thought to object.

Heading down the concourse to Gate B5, Andrea felt the weight of the satchel, which held her laptop computer and the four thick purchase agreements — each slightly different —

that she'd prepared for tomorrow's closing in Washington. This afternoon she'd devised a fifth option, but the legal department hadn't returned an approved version to her office before she left.

While sitting in traffic on the Kennedy Expressway, Andrea had decided the fifth option wouldn't work, but that didn't make any difference. If the new contract wasn't overnighted to her hotel in Washington, heads would roll. She'd see to that.

Her stride slowed as she approached a telephone bank. On a phone at the far end, facing her but not looking at her, was a man much taller than herself. He was 6-foot-4, well above her 5-foot-9, and she noticed that the public-phone handset looked child-sized in his hand. She also noted the brown hair and broad shoulders; the perfectly tailored, three-piece, charcoal suit; the red tie that wasn't subtle; and the wingtip shoes polished to a high shine.

He was in his late 30s, she guessed, noting a vitality that seemed at odds with the conservative suit. Very good-looking, Andrea thought as she continued on. That would have been interesting.

Walking into the waiting area at Gate B5, she joined the short line to the check-in counter and pulled her ticket from its usual slot in her briefcase. Her secretary, an irritatingly dull and dumpy girl, was at least efficient. But, with a few more closings like tomorrow's, Andrea would make it clear to the head of personnel that the secretary and her little bowl of fresh flowers had to go. Andrea wanted someone smart and attractive, who would serve as a reflection of herself, and it rankled that she hadn't received a new secretary when she'd first asked.

"Next!"

Andrea stepped forward and tossed her ticket onto the counter. The middle-aged woman wearing the airline's uniform gave Andrea a sharp look of assessment as she picked up the ticket, then asked for a photo ID.

"I want an upgrade," Andrea announced, pulling a frequent-flyer certificate from her wallet.

"First class is full," the woman replied. "I'm sorry." Her tone was polite but firm. "And you'll have to check one of your bags. Only two carry-ons are allowed."

Andrea tried to stare the woman down, but it did no good. Finally, she handed over the garment bag. The woman attached a tag and gave Andrea the claim ticket. "Next, please." The woman looked past Andrea, who had no excuse for not stepping aside, but made a point of not hurrying.

On board, Andrea settled into her window seat. The flight to D.C. would be one hour and 38 minutes, long enough for a full review of her notes and plans. Tomorrow's meeting would have no surprises — at least not for her. The three businessmen who'd built a nine-station radio network in the Washington-Virginia-Maryland area would come into the room with their lawyers, ready to sign the final papers. Then Andrea would tell them that the deal had changed.

She would explain that Chicago Radio Alliance's offer had

dropped from $85 to $80 million and that CRA wanted two years to pay the purchase price, not the agreed-upon six months. By itself, that would save CRA more than $6 million.

Andrea had done her homework, and she knew she had the upper hand. The three men were planning to buy a Baltimore television station, but their option on that deal expired in 10 days. If they wanted the TV station, they needed to sell the radio stations. They'd put themselves into a vise, and Andrea was going to give the handle a few turns.

The agreed-upon deal had been a good one for CRA, but her job was to make it better. At about 15 closings each year, Andrea would replace the usual negotiator for a final, unexpected confrontation. She had the performance down pat: "Our chief financial officer hit the roof when he saw this agreement ..." "To be honest, there's a radio network in New England that's a better fit for us ..." and the usual "We just can't justify this to our shareholders ..."

First would come the outraged response, then things would settle down and the sellers would usually make a few concessions to get the deal done.

And, with every closing, Andrea learned a little more.

Four years ago, she had gone to a closing in Pittsburgh, where she sat alone in a conference room with a bright-eyed 85-year-old named Edgar Pearce who'd decided that even he wasn't going to live forever. As part of his effort to avoid estate taxes, he was selling his 12-station radio network.

When Andrea said that her analysts had decided the network "just wasn't worth $60 million, and nothing above $50 million could be justified," Pearce had looked down at his hands for a long time, then called for a portable phone. In front of Andrea, he made a two-minute call to Dallas and sold the network for $60 million. When he finished, he rose and walked out of the room without another word to her.

The next day, after being lambasted by her boss ("Your job is to squeeze them a little, not blow the deal!"), Andrea learned that Pearce had made his first fortune in coal, then multiplied it a dozen times via honest but unyielding business negotiations. Everyone in western Pennsylvania knew that you didn't cross Edgar Pearce. Never again had Andrea gone to a closing without doing all her research.

From her satchel, she pulled out the computer and slipped it into the seat-back pouch in front of her. From her briefcase, she withdrew a heavy folder of notes, then put the satchel and briefcase at her feet.

"Pardon me, this is Row 22, isn't it?"

She looked up. The man from the telephone bank was looking down at her, smiling. Maybe I won't get so much work done after all, Andrea thought.

"This is it," she said, with a smile.

"Great." He took off his jacket, folded and stowed it in the overhead storage bin, and sat down in Seat B.

Andrea, without looking directly at his hands, saw there wasn't a gold band on his ring finger. She dropped her left hand down next to her knee, tucked her left thumbnail under her engagement ring, and nimbly worked the diamond solitaire off her finger.

Andrea purposely kept the ring a little loose, a precaution that in just six weeks had already proved useful. And she'd do the same with her wedding ring. So what if she had a little fun on the road? She wouldn't be the first; that was certain. What was the saying among foreign correspondents? "Wheels up, rings off." Andrea liked that.

Slipping the engagement ring into her jacket pocket, she opened her notes and, paying only half-attention to the words, waited for the inevitable interruption. Andrea guessed that he would ask about her computer or its software — those were the usual onboard conversation-starters. Instead, the man in Seat B closed his eyes.

He said nothing while the plane was pushed back from the gate, taxied out to the runway, took off, and climbed to 29,000 feet. Andrea was annoyed. She didn't think he was sleeping, and she wasn't used to being ignored. She was beautiful — in fact, "striking" was the word she heard most often — which was why she didn't understand the man next to her.

He'd made no attempt at eye contact; there had been no jokes, no conversation at all. Maybe his tastes didn't include women, she thought, then dismissed the idea. He'd noticed her looks; she was sure of it. His first glance had been too frank, too assessing. And, as he took his seat, she'd seen his eyes slide off her face and down.

Andrea looked at him again, allowing herself an up-close

47

stare that would have been rude if his eyes had been open. He was, she decided, even better-looking than she'd first thought. The brown hair was slightly curly and imperfectly combed, the button-down shirt was a crisp white, and the dark vest emphasized his shoulders.

As her gaze returned to his face, Andrea realized that his profile, handsome enough to be sculpted, had an appealing ruggedness. In fact, he reminded her of something ... Was it Michelangelo's *David* she wondered, as his head turned. Then his eyes opened, and she was caught looking straight at him from 18 inches away.

His smile was slow and amused. "So, how are you?"

"Good," she replied firmly, masking discomfort with assertiveness. "I'm very good."

"And what is making you so very good?" His voice was calm, the words measured. Oh, this one was sure of himself, Andrea thought. There was even a hint of taunt or tease in his voice. She hesitated. He had her off-balance.

"You were going to tell me what makes you so very good," prompted the man in Seat B.

If this was a negotiation, Andrea would have called for a break. She needed to regroup. She thought of telling him to get lost, but she didn't want this one to get lost. She didn't dare strike an attitude. Instead, she fell back on her "nice girl" act.

"Well, you caught me by surprise," Andrea replied, coming up with an embarrassed smile. Good work, she complimented herself, you almost sound bashful.

"Everyone's the same," said the man in Seat B. "People are what interest us most. We're always looking at each other. That's why there are sidewalk cafés in Paris."

"Have you spent much time there?" She reminded herself to keep smiling.

"A bit," he replied, enigmatically. "So, tell me about yourself."

"I'm a vice president at Chicago Radio Alliance, where I ..."

"No, no, tell me about you, not your job."

Andrea's mind stalled. Why didn't he want to hear about her work? Anger rose up in her, and she decided to challenge him, then immediately changed her mind. Wrong tactic. Don't win the battle and lose the war, she told herself.

Andrea looked around the edges of her life, searching for something to offer. "You mean, where am I from?"

"Sure, something like that."

His request, "Tell me about yourself," was, Andrea realized, like a brilliant opening move in chess: perfectly unrevealing. She considered inventing a different persona, but she'd have to remember every detail, and there was too much intelligence in those eyes. Andrea resorted to the truth.

"I'm from Milwaukee. I came to Chicago to go to Northwestern as an undergraduate, then I picked up a business degree at Kellogg."

The man in Seat B waited.

What does he want me to say? Andrea pictured the lines in lonely-hearts ads: "Loves walking on the beach, good wine, and dinner in front of the fire." Yeah, sure. Damn! Why doesn't he want to talk about politics or the economy or the president?

He helped her out. "Are you married?" he asked.

"No."

"I'm surprised."

"Too much work, too much travel," she said with a small shrug as she pictured Jonathan, her rich, eager-to-please fiancé. It had been a whirlwind courtship, carefully managed, of course. A week ago, during a passionate night, she'd convinced him that no prenuptial agreement was necessary. But his wealth, from the Dunsany fortune, was family money — it could run out. Now, if someone came along who generated a small fortune every year ... well, there was always time for a late entry to join the race.

"So, tell me about you," Andrea said. "Why were you in Paris?"

"It was back during college. I was going to the Sorbonne for a year."

"Then your French must be perfect." Her tone emphasized the compliment.

"Not at first. When I arrived, I realized my French was terrible, but I didn't want to learn academic French; I'd just sound like a student. I wanted the real language, the way it's spoken in the streets. When I was a kid, I learned some magic tricks, so in Paris I put together a magic act and performed down in the Metro stations and on street corners. The magician's patter draws a crowd, and then they talk back to you. You learn fast."

Not too glamorous, Andrea thought, disappointed. But he certainly had an aura of success about him now. "You don't look like you've been standing out on many street corners lately."

"No, I'm a surgeon. Cardiac, mainly. Same hands, different tricks."

"Really!" Andrea exclaimed. "You must tell me all about it!" And, for the remainder of the flight, they talked. Andrea tried to keep the conversation centered on him, but it often was deflected back to her. She didn't learn as much as she wanted, but she laughed, smiled, and made sure that once her knee touched his, the contact was maintained. Nor was Andrea's interest feigned because, as they talked, she became more and more aware of him physically.

She made her decision as the plane began its descent into Dulles. Andrea asked if he knew of any good restaurants in Washington that would be open after 9 p.m.

"A few," he said, understanding the opening he'd been given. He looked at her in reappraisal. "Would you care to have dinner?"

"I'd love to!"

"Then I think I can promise you a memorable one."

"Good," she said with a long look, "and I can promise

you a memorable evening."

As the plane landed and taxied to the terminal, there was no more need to talk. Andrea was pleased — their negotiation was complete and the bargain had been struck, though not in so many words, of course.

They disembarked together and, while walking through the first concourse, discussed the best French restaurants in the D.C. area. They passed gift shops and newsstands, but it was a closed flower shop that served as a reminder to the man who'd known to ask for Row 22, Seat B. Tomorrow, a bowl of fresh flowers would be delivered to the desk of a certain secretary in the Amoco Building.

At Dulles' main terminal, Andrea said that she needed to pick up her bag.

"Fine. I'll call Chez François and meet you at baggage claim."

Andrea gave him her sexiest smile and turned toward the baggage carousels. "Wait," he said, putting out his right hand, "I guess we should introduce ourselves. My name is Edward Dunsany."

"I'm Andrea ..." His name clicked into place. "... Bain ..." she finished dully, her voice trailing off. "You're ..."

"Jonathan's brother? Yes, I am."

Andrea put on her biggest smile. "Well, gosh! We're almost family!" Arms wide, she stepped forward and gave Edward a hug, trying to bluff her way out.

It was just what he guessed she would do. When Andrea

stepped back, there was only cold detachment in Edward Dunsany's eyes.

"We aren't family, and we never will be," he said with unemotional finality. "My younger brother is deeply in love with you, but he's not a fool. Someone told him that you travel with his engagement ring in your pocket. You told him that you love him. He didn't know who to believe. You just answered the question for him."

Andrea searched for a plausible lie, but she'd already lost, and she knew it. Damn! All that money — gone! No, not all of it. She pulled the engagement ring out of her jacket pocket and jammed it onto her left ring finger.

"That's a family ring," Edward said evenly. "It's not yours to keep."

"Then you can just sue me for it," Andrea replied defiantly. "You're not getting it now." With a dismissive toss of her head, she turned away and marched down the corridor, high heels clicking against the floor tiles.

Edward walked out the automatic doors to the taxi stand. He stepped into the first cab. "Fairfax, please," he said to the driver. "319 Center Street."

As the cab pulled away, Edward took out a cellular phone and punched in a series of numbers.

"Hello," answered a voice back in Chicago.

"Jonathan, it's Edward."

There was a hesitation. "How was your trip?"

"Not so good. I did what you wanted, and I'm afraid you

were right — you never could have trusted her. I'm sorry."

Jonathan's slow exhale was audible over the phone. Edward could imagine his brother, leaner and shorter than himself, running a hand through his blond hair, trying to accept the unwanted fact.

"And the ring?" Jonathan asked finally.

"She's not about to give it back."

With his free hand, Edward reached into his jacket pocket and withdrew a diamond solitaire that, even in the taxi's darkness, drew light to its prisms. It was as beautiful as the insurance photos showed — photos so good that a duplicate could easily be made.

"Jonathan, tell me, have you ever noticed how much those cubic-zirconia fakes look like real diamonds?"

"No, not really. Why? The diamond I gave her was real; you know that ..." Jonathan paused. Then, with a little more life in his voice, he asked, "Edward, has the Paris street magician pulled off one more trick?"

"Let's just say that a few minutes ago, Andrea gave me a very expensive hug."

"I owe you a lot, big brother."

"Actually, the ring was only $48.90. But, I promise you, Jonathan, it's the bargain of a lifetime." ♦

Musical Chairs

A llan Cochran, humming softly to himself, arrived at San Francisco Airport's Gate 84 check-in counter at the same moment as a pale, harassed-looking woman.

"You first," he smiled, stepping back.

"Are you sure?" She held up a thick, brown envelope. "I'm checking in 122 people."

"You're very persuasive," Allan said, handing his ticket folder and photo ID to the ticket agent. He turned back to the woman. "Is this a group tour or just a very big family?"

"Both. It's the Philadelphia Symphony Orchestra. We finished a concert tour in the Far East yesterday. If you can imagine how grumpy any family would be after 19 cities in 21 days, you've got the right idea."

"The harmony's gone?"

"Almost all of it. There's a rumor that two of the trumpeters are still talking to each other, but it hasn't been confirmed." The gate attendant, a short, blond man with an ill-advised mustache, stamped a boarding pass, slipped it into Allan's ticket folder, and returned it, along with the ID. "You'll be in Row 22, Seat B, sir."

"You're taking the place of our top violinist," said the woman with the envelope.

"Pardon?" Allan replied.

"For three weeks, 22B has been Jacob Elston's seat. Everyone gets the same seat for the whole tour; it's less confusing that way. But Jacob flew down to Los Angeles early this morning for some recording work — on a film score, I think. You'll be sitting next to his wife, Jessica, who is both a great cellist and the nicest person in the whole orchestra. You'll enjoy talking to her."

From the concourse behind them, a heavily accented voice boomed, "Has anyone seen one of our road managers? I'd trade them all for a good horn player. Of course, I'd trade anything for a good horn player."

Out in the corridor stood a tall man with approximately 25 people gathered around him. His hair, mustache, and goatee were all of the same devil-red hue, giving him a commanding, almost forbidding presence.

"Our fearless leader," the woman said without turning to look. "He's had a case of the sniffles and probably wants a tissue."

"A difficult man?" asked Allan.

"Miklós Jékely needs an extra seat just for his ego."

"Who is he, your conductor?"

Her weary expression eased into a half-smile. "Miklós would be devastated to hear that someone on his planet doesn't know him."

Allan shrugged. "I like jazz — Ellington, Beiderbecke, Miles Davis. I'm afraid that Beethoven, Mozart, and all the rest of them just sound the same to me."

Her smile broadened. "Would you mind coming over and saying that to Miklós? In front of his adoring fans? It would be the highlight of my year!"

"Thanks for the offer, but I've learned to let sleeping dogs lie."

"Too bad. He throws great tantrums — some of the best I've seen."

Allan regarded the famous conductor and realized that there was, in fact, something familiar about him. That was how fame worked, Allan thought, someone's image is recycled through newspapers, magazines, and television until anonymity becomes awareness, then recognition, and finally fame. The familiar stranger — another product of the modern world.

Boarding began a few minutes later, and Allan found himself sitting next to a woman who offered a sweet smile as he sat down. Jessica Elston, slender with light-brown hair that just brushed her shoulders, had a calm, untroubled face. If Allan hadn't already heard about her, he might have guessed that she was an attractive grade-school teacher on vacation.

Thirty minutes later, after the plane reached its cruising altitude of 33,000 feet, several passengers got up to walk around the cabin, including a pear-shaped man with white hair who stopped next to Row 22.

"Good luck tomorrow, Jessica."

She looked up. "Thanks, John."

"You'll be the best player at the audition — no one has a sound like yours. 'Jékely-and-Hyde' ought to be begging you to take over first chair."

"You don't have any incriminating photos I can use, do you?"

"I wish I did, but regardless of who he chooses, you deserve it."

"That's kind of you to say, John."

"It's the truth," he replied, and moved down the aisle.

Jessica glanced at Allan. "We're all part of an orchestra," she offered in explanation.

"The Philadelphia Symphony, I was told." He related some of what he'd learned at the check-in counter. "But there's something I don't understand: If you're already in the orchestra, why are you auditioning?"

"Our principal cellist is retiring, and the auditions are to decide who replaces him." She paused and, not receiving a nod of understanding from her seatmate, continued, "The principal cellist gets all the solos and is recognized as the best player in that section."

"Then I hope you get the job."

"I won't."

"But, from what your friend said, you must have a pretty good chance."

"No," she said simply, "in truth, I have no chance at all. Miklós doesn't pick women for the principal chairs."

"How can he do that?"

"The judging at auditions is totally subjective, and his opinion is the only one that's important." Her tone was matter-of-fact, but there was a trace of something else in her voice. "Miklós can claim that someone else's bow work is crisper, that their fingerwork is better, or that they have a richer vibrato."

"Isn't there someone you can complain to?"

"No. We're the serfs in Miklós' kingdom."

"Could you take him to court?"

"Miklós is too smart to say out loud that no woman will ever sit in a principal's chair in his orchestra. And how could a judge or jury say that his choice of one musician over another was wrong? Could you imagine 10 professional cellists playing, one after another, in a courtroom? An ordinary person would never hear the difference."

Jessica shook her head. "Also, I'd have to keep working for him while I was suing him. It wouldn't be much fun, and I don't have the stomach for years of animosity. Maybe someone else can pressure Miklós, but I don't know anything about infighting, politics, or how to put the squeeze on people. I just play the cello."

"What's it like playing for him?" Allan asked.

Jessica sighed and smiled at the same time. "That's what makes it even harder. You see, he's brilliant! In the 12 years since he took over the PhilSym, he's rebuilt it into one of the world's best. When he stands up on the podium, he knows what he wants from each musician. Miklós has memorized every note of every composition, and he acts as if he just got off the phone with the composer, who told him how each note should be played.

"If we're doing Dvořák's Sixth, in the opening he knows just how to soften the syncopated chords of D major. Or in Brahms' First, he understands how to turn the harmony. He's the only person on the stage who doesn't make a sound, but he's controlling the phrasing of every instrument, balancing the strings against the horns, and making sure that every measure fits into the whole piece. My husband says that playing for Jékely is like being a racehorse ridden by the world's greatest jockey, who knows how to get the best out of you, and you'd die for him during a race, but, off the track, you'd always be looking to take a bite out of his shoulder.

"Miklós converts a hundred musicians into one big instrument; then he plays us just the way he wants, and we think we're lucky to be there! A compliment from him, even if it's just a nod of approval, is like gold. If someone makes a mistake, even a slightly ragged sixteenth note, he'll hear it. He can be facing the basses, on his right, and if one of 25 violinists behind him screws up, he'll turn around and look at exactly who did it. Oh, he drives us all crazy, but we wouldn't want to play for anyone else."

"Where's he from?"

"Hungary. There's this myth that to be a great conductor, you must be from Europe, especially Eastern Europe. Because of the accent, they seem more exotic, more mysterious I guess. You see, audiences want more than just a symphony and a few sonatas; they want to be entertained, and Miklós does that. During a performance, he's up there demanding, coaxing, and pleading with us; we provide the music, and he provides the theater. Trust me, there's never going to be a conductor of a major American orchestra who has a Bronx or Boston accent and looks like your neighbor."

"Your friend called him 'Jékely-and-Hyde.'"

"Miklós is probably the most complex person I've ever met. He can summon up the sweetness of angels when a piece calls for it — then an hour later, he'll fire the stage manager. But, to be honest, he's not simply a Dr. Jekyll and Mr. Hyde. I admire Miklós because he's gone beyond just being a musician; he's a businessman who understands perfectly the politics of the classical-music business. Someone said that every time he starts a negotiation, whether it's for a record, for a tour, or to be a guest conductor, he's already got the playing field tilted in his favor.

"I admire his talent," she continued, "but I admire his

nerve even more. I'm good at concerts, not confrontations. I don't like Miklós, but I'll tell you the truth — I'd love to be him for a day, just to see what it's like."

Allan looked at the woman next to him, at the lips pressed firmly together and the determination now revealed in her eyes. There, he realized, was the drive that makes a musician great, and, intuitively, he understood that she could only have married someone who also had it.

"I was told that your husband is the best violinist in the orchestra."

"He's the concertmaster — that means he's the principal violinist," Jessica said, her mood visibly lightening. "And I love listening to him." She paused, then with a hint of embarrassment continued her thought. "To tell you the truth, I fell in love with him before I ever heard him say a word. Ten years ago, before he joined the orchestra, he came to Philadelphia as a guest soloist.

"Maybe an audience never thinks about it, but we're not musicians just because we have a knack for it — it's not like becoming an accountant simply because you're good at math. We love the music. Making works of genius come out of our hands and our lips — that's why we spent our childhoods practicing alone in a room. I sat across the stage from Jacob and listened to him play Vaughan Williams' *Lark Ascending* and I cried all the way through — it was that beautiful. Six months later, he played with us again, and I made sure that I met him."

"Not many people love their work," Allan said.

"And what do you do?"

"Nothing like that. I sell insurance — home, auto, and theft policies, mainly. It's not too glamorous; there aren't many tours of the Far East. I live in the same town I grew up in, down the California coast, south of San Francisco, in Monterey."

"And do you like selling insurance?"

"Honestly? Yes. It suits me. Everyone's brain is wired a little differently. You were given the talent to play music; I have a memory for names and faces. My wife calls it a 'salesman's memory,' and she swears that I've never forgotten anyone I ever met. When I walk down the street and meet a dozen of my policyholders, I can greet every one of them by name. That's why I keep their business."

"And what's in Philadelphia?"

Allan explained that his only time away from Monterey was four years of college in Philadelphia, where he met his wife. This weekend would be their 20th anniversary, and he'd booked four nights at the Latham, in the same suite where they spent their honeymoon. "Irene went back a few days early to see her family."

As they talked, lunch was served, then the in-flight movie began, and Jessica, who'd started the previous day eight time zones away, immediately fell asleep. She did not stir for two hours, until the window shades were raised and midafternoon sunshine filled the cabin.

At the front of the coach section, the blue curtain was yanked aside and Miklós Jékely, looking neither left nor right, marched down the aisle. Allan, interested to see the conductor close-up, looked at him with curiosity; then, as he drew closer, Allan's eyes narrowed. Jékely swept past, continued to the back of the plane, and entered a lavatory.

"Miklós doesn't wait for anyone," said Jessica, blinking as her eyes adapted to the sunlight.

Allan turned and looked back down the aisle where Jékely had disappeared. After a long minute, he said, "I know him."

"What?"

"Jékely, your conductor. I know him."

"Of course. He's famous."

"No, no, I've met him, I remember him."

"From where?"

"School."

"In Philadelphia?"

"No. Grade school, back in California."

"You're wrong. Miklós grew up in Hungary."

"Your Miklós has mean little eyes," Allan said.

"Yes, he does."

"Well, for three years I went to school with a kid who had those same eyes. And he had red hair. He was obnoxious and overbearing, and he went home every day to practice the piano, which he played very, very well."

"But, you'd remember if his name was Miklós Jékely!"

"It wasn't. His parents wanted very much to fit in with everyone in town. They were the Kellys, and they moved away when their son Mike was about 12 years old."

"And Mike Kelly became Miklós Jékely?" Jessica's skepticism was evident.

Allan looked down the aisle just as Jékely emerged from the lavatory. An elderly woman was slowly making her way toward the back of the plane, so Jékely crossed over to the aisle on the far side and strode back up to first class.

Jessica looked at Allan.

"I'm not sure," he shrugged. "I could be wrong."

They talked for the last half-hour of the flight, though Allan's attention wandered as he struggled to add 30 years, a mustache, and goatee to an old memory. He wavered, doubting himself — but, still, there was something ...

After landing, during disembarkation, Allan hoped for another look at the conductor but didn't see him again. "Whisked to his limo," Jessica commented as they walked together through the terminal. "Miklós gets a lot of limos. It's in his contract." In the manner of many airplane conversations, they introduced themselves as they said good-bye.

Two days later, on Sunday morning, Allan was humming to himself as he took a long, hot shower in the memory-filled suite of the Latham. He heard the bathroom door open, then the shower door, and Irene, wearing a white, terry-cloth robe, stood in the escaping steam, smiling, a champagne bottle in one hand. Allan looked at his wife and grinned.

"You didn't have enough of that last night?"

"I didn't order it."

"What's it doing here?"

Irene pulled a white envelope from the pocket of her robe. "This was taped to the bottle."

Allan turned off the shower and, with a large bath towel, dried his head and hands before taking the envelope. He pulled the tape off the back and withdrew a newspaper clipping that, unfolded, revealed the headline: "Jékely Names First Female Principal."

The story's opening paragraphs were: "Miklós Jékely, long-rumored to have a policy against appointing any woman as a principal player with the Philadelphia Symphony, silenced his critics Saturday by naming Jessica Elston as principal cellist.

"Jékely praised Elston's talent, knowledge, and experience with the orchestra. 'She was clearly the best candidate,' he said. Elston, when asked about her appointment as the orchestra's first female leader of a section, commented, 'I'm sure I won't be the last.'"

Allan, smiling, skimmed the rest of the story, then handed it to his wife. He looked in the envelope again and withdrew two tickets and a short note with eight words written on it: "Thanks. The playing field was level this time."

"Would you like to go to the symphony tonight?" Allan asked Irene as he put the tickets on the sink and continued to dry himself.

"Classical music's not exactly your style."

"No, but I'd like to go this time."

Allan wondered how Jessica had let her conductor know that this audition, and all those in the future, were going to be fair. Perhaps a casual reference to Monterey and an admirer named Allan Cochran, then Jessica would have begun her audition. Jékely, suddenly wary of this calm, quiet woman, would have wondered whether he'd been given a compliment or a warning, and as she played on, a silent negotiation would have taken place between them. Jékely, uncertain whether Jessica was innocent or shrewd, would have weighed his bias against his career and decided he couldn't take the chance. If she was the best, she'd have to win.

"The champagne and tickets are thank-you presents," Allan explained.

"Then the conductor you told me about, that Kelly-Jékely guy, he was your old classmate?"

"It was him all right, but the gifts are from a woman who plays for him. A very nice woman, in fact, who found out yesterday that she's just as adept at politics as she is at playing the cello." ♦

Trust Me

"The sense of betrayal was the hardest thing to deal with," I said.

"Your father always knew it would be," replied Jean-Louis Bertrand, my late father's lawyer. "And that was the hardest part for him, too. We talked about it for many, many hours."

I was sitting next to Bertrand on the late-afternoon flight from Paris to Zürich.

"You talked more with my father than I ever did."

"That is probably true."

"And shared more secrets."

"That is certainly true."

"Secrets that I'm never going to learn about."

"That was your father's request."

I glanced at the man in Seat B. He was in his early 60s, wore wire-rim glasses, and had on a dark-blue suit, white shirt, and perfectly knotted tie. M. Bertrand sat with his hands clasped before him, fingers interlocked. His appearance was as precise as his words.

"You knew everything that was going to happen, didn't you, Monsieur Bertrand?"

"Yes, I did."

"Was it your idea?"

"No. When your father called me about this, he didn't ask for my opinion; he simply gave me instructions."

"And it all happened as he expected?"

"Yes. You were the only uncertainty — at least, that's what I thought. But your father told me, in fact, that you were the one certainty. He was absolutely sure of you."

The words pleased me, for I am, like all other sons, attuned to any compliment from my father.

Bertrand continued, "Because of a letter, he said that he had no doubt about you. I believe he wrote it when you were quite young."

"I was 15," I answered. "We weren't on speaking terms then — I don't remember why."

But I did remember the letter, left on my pillow one night. I remember because it was the foundation for our future relationship. It was the reaching out of a wise father to a difficult son. Over the years, I've read those five sentences so many times that I've memorized them.

"Henri — I don't know which it is, that we are too different or we are too similar, but I fear that we will

fail as father and son. We have fought and argued for too long, and so I suggest a truce. What I offer are two things: a promise that I will never lie to you, and a promise that I will never be unfair to you. In return, I only ask one thing — that you trust me. I won't ask for your love, and I won't even ask that you like me, but in those days or years that you hate me, if you trust me, we will never lose each other."

And my father's instinct proved correct. Holding on to those words, we reached a middle ground that was tentatively approached then firmly claimed. I believe that he never lied to me, and, until he died, I never had reason to think he had been unfair. So I trusted him, and it was out of that trust that I came to love him.

I remember my father's long, laughing conversations with my mother and Bertrand, his two closest friends. He and I could never talk that way; our words and thoughts never seemed to blend, but, because of his letter, we became the closest of strangers.

But these three months since his death had thrown me back into an almost adolescent roller coaster of emotions. I was disappointed and hurt, angry at him and angry at myself. I felt betrayed and foolish for having trusted him so much.

"Your response was crucial," continued Bertrand. "I was struck by how much faith your father put in you. He said that the two of you had an agreement, and that despite every

71

appearance, every circumstance, you'd keep your word."

Blind faith, I thought. Everyone needs to believe in something, and the first thing that children believe in is their parents. We don't want them to be fallible, but finally we yield and let them be human.

I never knew all the corners of my father's life. I did know that he was born in Switzerland, moved to France in his early 20s, and quickly made a fortune leasing and subleasing commercial properties. His business interests branched out and eventually reached around the world, from Singapore to Miami and Oslo to Johannesburg, where he met the young woman who became my mother.

Much of my father's success was due to an odd quirk of visual imagination, for he could correctly predict the direction and timing of a young city's growth. He could see where and when, pressured by population and industry, a city would break through its boundaries. My father would rent a small plane and fly over a city for hours, first recognizing why the earliest settlement had been placed there. Then, in ever-widening circles, he would gradually work his way out, studying the roads, the rivers, and the contours of the land until he could picture the next, inevitable surge of expansion.

He would buy several large properties, usually farms that could be rented back to the farmers for a few more years, until the businessmen without foresight arrived, ready to pay 50- or 100-fold for their sudden need to build roads, homes, and stores. My father would sell and move on.

And there were other businesses, highly profitable ones, that my father would not talk about, though I knew they involved oddly circuitous routes for imports and exports. These profits were quickly converted into invisible investments, specifically diamonds, rare stamps, and coins that would appear in no bank account, stock portfolio, or corporate record. And this portion of my father's wealth grew without a taxable trace. Because of his visual imagination, it was perhaps inevitable that he would develop an interest in art. Over the next 20 years, the diamonds, stamps, and coins were converted into nearly 100 extraordinary paintings.

Other works — sketches, drawings, and sculptures — were on display throughout the house, but the paintings were all held in one wing, carefully framed and hung in two large rooms, where my father could often be found sitting in front of any one painting for an hour or more. I once asked him why, and he explained, "With a bad artist, in five minutes you'll see everything that he put into the painting. With a genius, the longer you look, the more you see."

I did not have my father's eye for art, but there was one picture I grew to love. It was by Canfield, a little-known English painter of the 1800s, and showed two burly workmen sitting atop a partially built stone wall, rocks strewn about their feet. Their hats pushed back on their heads, they were eating a simple meal of bread and cheese and talking to each other. Both men, eyes twinkling, were on the verge of laughter. I understood myself well enough to know why I liked Canfield's painting so much.

My father's judgment on all things business was perfect. The only major mistake that he made in his life was understandable, for it has been made by thousands of other widowers. The young woman looked just like my mother had at the age of 30. Blonde and slender with soft blue eyes, she even spoke with the same gentle South African accent.

Sylvia was indeed beautiful, and her charm pulled my father ever deeper in love. Their courtship was quick and the marriage inevitable. I was my father's best man, and I was glad to be, for I, too, had been fooled. It was more than a year before his first doubt formed; then he became more alert to her words and actions and realized that she was not in love with him and never had been. My father had been convenient, as rich men often are, and he knew that every morning he was waking up next to a woman who didn't love him. Sylvia, sensing his awareness, stopped putting up any pretense.

She did not cheat on him — under French law, that would have jeopardized the marriage. As M. Bertrand explained to my father, as long as Sylvia committed no overt acts and remained "an innocent party," she could delay a divorce for six years and thus remain the cosseted wife of a multimillionaire. Whichever path my father chose would be an expensive one, but before he could make his choice, the fates intervened.

Cancer of the pancreas is brutally swift. The first diagnosis gave him three months; the second opinion gave him two. And, as he wasted away, I never saw a moment's grief in

Sylvia's eyes. Her timing had been impeccable. Marry a rich man; then watch him die — it was the dream of every black widow.

I never asked my father why he hadn't required a prenuptial agreement from Sylvia, but he offered an answer anyway. "I thought I'd found your mother again — and I couldn't imagine her being dishonest."

During my father's last months, I visited as often as my schedule, that of a university assistant professor, would allow. And I saw how much time Sylvia spent in the paintings' wing. She had no love for the art, only for its value, and she knew how much my father had paid for each work. She figured, rightly, that their total worth would be between 240 and 330 million francs, depending upon how much excitement was generated by their auction.

In the art world, there are always doubts and suspicions because fakes have tricked even the best art experts, but microscopes do not lie. It was Bertrand who suggested a scientific testing of the collection to confirm the age of each work, and Sylvia immediately championed this idea. Microscopic specks of paint, taken from beneath the pictures' frames, were sent to a laboratory in London that specialized in spectroscopic analysis.

One week later, the test results were returned. My father's eye for genius had been validated. Every picture was genuine.

During my father's illness, I often sat with him, and each day, no matter how weak he felt, he would ask to go to the paintings' wing. There was nothing to him by then, so we did not bother with wheelchairs and elevators. I would pick him up and carry him downstairs, where he would name a picture — occasionally the Canfield — and I would place him in a chair before it. He would sit there, studying his familiar friend until he drifted off; then I'd return him to his bed.

I could not be at my father's side every day, nor could Bertrand, but Sylvia was always there. For two months, she drilled into my father that he owed her complete security for the rest of her life, that it was his duty to take care of her, telling him that she'd given up her career for him. When I arrived at the house, it was often to the sound of her raised voice, telling my father what she "deserved."

During his last two days, sedated by painkillers, my father drifted in and out of consciousness as I sat next to his bed, holding his hand. One afternoon, when I thought he was asleep, he gripped my hand with sudden strength, and his eyes opened with absolute clarity.

"Do you still trust me?" His voice was an intense whisper.

"I always have."

"Don't ever stop."

I hid my confusion and gave him my word. After a long moment, my father's hand lost its strength again and his eyes faded back into bleary confusion. Four hours later, I took my hand from his, for he was no longer there.

It was five days later that Sylvia, her lawyer, and I sat in

M. Bertrand's office for the reading of the will.

What I remember most from that morning was Sylvia's joy. M. Bertrand, in his clear, clipped way, read aloud my father's words, which bequeathed to Sylvia the whole art collection, including Canfield's workmen. She had worn my father down and won. M. Bertrand continued, saying that 180,000 francs had been set aside for Sylvia's immediate use and that death duties would be paid by the sale of my father's house and land. The remainder of his estate, consolidated into one account at the Banque Nationale de Paris, would be mine. The math was simple: Depending upon what the paintings brought at auction, Sylvia's share would be six to eight times what I received.

The final clause provided a three-month window for challenges by Sylvia or me. The paintings would be placed in a bank vault, and there would be no distributions until we both signed an irrevocable agreement accepting our shares.

Sylvia conferred in a whisper with her lawyer, then announced, "We can take care of this right now. I have no disagreement with the will. I think it's very fair." She turned to me. "Are you going to contest your father's wishes?"

I was still too stunned to answer. "I'll reserve my right," was all I managed to say.

"This is what he wanted!" Sylvia had instantly adopted the righteous tone of the loyal widow.

"I'll reserve my right," I repeated.

She whispered again with her lawyer, who kept glancing

at me and shaking his head. I guessed she was asking whether I could be forced to sign before the three months elapsed.

Bertrand, who had been named executor, said he would prepare an acceptance agreement that would be ready at our mutual convenience. Sylvia, without another word, stood up, directed a look of sneering disdain at me, and departed with her lawyer.

I looked at Bertrand. "This isn't what I expected."

"I know," he nodded.

"I'm willing to fight her."

"Your father hoped to spare you that battle."

"So he gave her everything she wanted!" I thought of Canfield's workmen and already missed them. I'd never asked, and my father had never promised, but I'd always hoped that I, too, would grow old looking at them.

"It doesn't seem fair," said Bertrand, "and it probably isn't. But your father understood that Sylvia is an accomplished and convincing liar. On the stand, she would cry and sob and play to perfection the role of the grieving widow, while subtly casting you as the greedy, grasping son. Remember, her pretense of love was so convincing that your father married her."

I looked at my copy of the will and saw that it was dated six weeks ago. "Do you believe that my father was of sound mind when he wrote this?"

"Honestly, I do," replied Bertrand. "I was present when he signed it. His mind and judgment were perfect. That's what I would have to testify to."

I left M. Bertrand's office and walked down rue de Galimon, then turned north on boulevard St-Michel, passed over l' Ile de la Cité, and spent the rest of the day walking, thinking, and struggling to fit my father's final act to the truce we'd both lived by.

The extra money wasn't important; I would be rich enough. It was the betrayal of trust that took so long to accept. I needed the full three months to make peace with my father's decision.

An appointment was made with Bertrand. When I arrived, Sylvia's lawyer was already reviewing the agreement. When he finished, he looked at Sylvia and handed her a pen. She signed her name in the two required places. When I added my signatures, Sylvia officially became one of the wealthiest women in France.

Bertrand explained that it would take a few days to re-register the paintings in Sylvia's name, then she could remove them from the bank vault and decide whether she wished to sell or keep them.

"Oh, of course I'm going to keep them." Her tone was mocking. "I love good art."

Bertrand did not react. He turned to me. "The account at BNP may be transferred at your convenience. Where do you wish the money to be sent?" I handed him a sheet of paper with wiring instructions. "Then I believe that we are finished," Bertrand concluded.

"It's been a pleasure," Sylvia said, and marched out in triumph, her lawyer in her wake.

I remained seated in Bertrand's office. "I still don't believe it," I said finally.

"Don't dwell on it," he replied. "Your father believed this was for the best." Then he firmly turned the conversation in another direction. "Have you decided where you will scatter your father's ashes?"

"Yes. Outside Zürich, on the same mountain where he and I took my mother's ashes."

"When will you go?"

"Tomorrow or the next day." A trip, a change of some kind, would be good.

"If I might ask," said Bertrand, "I'd like to be there, too. It would mean a great deal to me. Could you wait 10 days?"

I didn't want to, but I could not refuse my father's friend.

"Thank you," he said. "And will you stay in Paris until then?"

I replied that I probably would.

It was three days later that *Le Monde* reported the first letter, sent to a family in Salzburg. The next day came reports of a dozen more letters, received in Bruges, Weisbaden, Marseilles, and Amsterdam. The following day, two dozen letters were delivered in the States. Every letter was addressed to a family and began with the same sentences: "During World War II, your family owned a beautiful painting that was stolen by the Third Reich. Your painting is now in the possession of a woman in Paris ..."

None of the nearly 100 letters was signed, but every letter was correct: All the pictures had been stolen, and Sylvia was the registered owner of every one of them. For the next week, the police and the press came to me and asked what I knew about my father's collection. I told them the truth, and they recognized my innocence; the problem, they decided, was not mine. Sylvia responded with defiant claims that every painting was legally hers. By the end of the 10 days, more than four dozen lawsuits had been lodged against her, including one that sought return of the Canfield. Later, I would ask M. Bertrand to inquire whether the picture might be for sale.

I looked out the airplane's window at the majestic range of Switzerland's Jura Mountains. In a bag tucked beneath the seat was a heavy square box. Tomorrow, perhaps at dawn, M. Bertrand and I would travel south of Zürich, to the top of the Uetliberg, and, when the morning breeze picked up, I would put my father's ashes into the air.

"There is one last thing," said M. Bertrand, reaching into his jacket pocket. "This is for you."

I opened the flap of the white envelope, preparing myself for the familiar handwriting. I opened the folded page.

"Henri — Because this is in your hand, everything must have gone right, and I apologize for what I've put you through. You know about the paintings now, and I

am embarrassed for having held them so long, know-ing they were not mine. In my defense, I can only say that I made a deal with myself: I could buy and keep those wonderful works only if, at my death, they were returned to their rightful owners. When Sylvia showed who she really was, I was forced to add another step to their return. Bertrand did not like my new plan. He was worried for you, but I told him not to be, for the only things that I'm sure of in this world are that my son knows I will never lie to him and that I will never be unfair to him. And I know that he'll always trust me. I love you, Your Father." ♦

Brother and Sister

"Stop it! Right now!"

The voice cut through all conversation at Denver International's Gate B46. Every face turned toward the center of the waiting area.

"Doesn't your mother ever make you behave?"

The harsh words, at odds with the man's conservative business suit, were aimed across the aisle at two children fighting for an armrest. The boy, who looked to be about nine, and the girl, perhaps a few years younger, shared the same fair skin and auburn hair.

"Put your hands in your laps!"

The children, both neatly dressed, glanced at each other.

"Now!" their father ordered, oblivious to the watching eyes and the growing silence around him.

The children obeyed.

He leaned forward, pointing a finger. "When you get off that plane, you tell your mother just how badly you behaved this week! Do you understand?"

Both children nodded.

He glared at them for a long moment, then took a newspaper from the seat next to him, shook it open, and snapped it once to take out the creases. He raised the paper, making a wall between him and the children, and began reading. Bystanders looked uncomfortably at each other, glanced at the now-still children, and turned away.

Rachel Scott, waiting in line at the check-in counter, did not look away. She saw the boy reach his right hand across his body and, from his hip, pull out a long, imaginary sword, point it at the newspaper, and slash a Z into the back of the pages. Young Zorro triumphantly slammed his sword back into its sheath, then grinned at his sister. She giggled.

The newspaper jerked down, but the two children were staring straight ahead, hands in their laps, all humor gone. With no excuse to reprimand them, their father could only glare at them.

Little survivors, Rachel thought. He hadn't been able to break them.

A tall girl with chestnut hair hurried into the waiting area for Gate B46 and stopped next to Rachel. "You won't believe what I found at the newsstand!"

Rachel looked into the green eyes that were now level

with her own. This was taking some getting used to, she thought. The child who'd fallen asleep on her shoulder a thousand times was now 5-foot-7 and pretty enough to turn heads when she walked through a crowd.

"What did you get?"

"The absolute best movie encyclopedia!" Clare held up a thick, paperback book. "Every movie ever made is in here! And there's an index for all the stars and directors!"

"Great," Rachel said, "but I don't need it. Whenever I want to know something, I just ask you."

"I don't know everything."

"Oh? Who was in *Cimarron Star*?"

"Robert Hutchins and Julia Morrison," Clare shrugged. "With John Fletcher as the bad guy."

"And who directed *Yesterday Lost*? Michael Isaacs or Aaron Whitfield?"

Clare laughed. "Too easy. Give me something harder."

"What year was *Mr. Paradise* made?"

"Trick question. Made in '81 but not released until '84 because the studio went bankrupt."

Rachel smiled. "My daughter, the walking encyclopedia."

Visibly pleased, Clare began skimming through the book. Rachel looked past her daughter at the children sitting in obedient silence. So familiar, she thought. Too familiar.

At the first boarding call, their father tossed the newspaper onto the next chair and stood up. His children understood the implicit command and got up, pulled their knapsacks from under their seats, and followed him to the gate.

At the door to the jetway, their boarding passes were checked and handed to the father, who gave the ticket folders to the boy. "Don't lose these or they'll throw you off the plane." The little girl moved a half-step closer to her brother. Rachel was aware that Clare was now watching.

One of the gate attendants, a short woman with a round, friendly face, stepped forward and said to the father, "Good morning. I'll take them on board and get them settled for you."

"Wonderful." The word was loaded with sarcasm. Rachel couldn't guess his business, but she was sure that his secretary hated him.

"And who will be meeting them in Los Angeles?" The gate attendant's tone was determinedly pleasant.

"Their mother's supposed to be there. If she doesn't show up, I guess they're your problem."

The gate attendant turned to the children. "Do you live in Los Angeles?"

They said they did.

"Good! So, if the pilot needs any directions, he can come back and ask you?"

"Oh, yes," the little girl nodded confidently.

"Excellent, I'll tell him that."

The gate attendant looked at the father, then stepped back so that he could give his children a hug or kiss good-bye.

"Do what you're told. And try not to be little jerks," he

said, then turned and walked away. The gate attendant stared at his back for only a second; then she smiled at the children and took the little girl's hand. "Off we go," she said, and the three of them headed down the ramp.

"Wow!" Clare said softly. "Is that guy human?"

"Barely," Rachel replied, watching to see if the father would look back. He turned a corner and disappeared.

"I hope their mother's nicer to them than he is," Clare said.

"I guess we'll know in a couple of hours."

A few minutes later, mother and daughter boarded the flight and found their seats in Row 22, across the aisle from the children. The little girl was in Seat A, next to the window, and her brother was in Seat B. On the armrest between them lay an open picture book. The boy was reading aloud.

"'The children waited in the classroom for Miss Johnson, and they waited and they waited ...'"

But his sister wasn't looking at the book — she knows every word and picture by heart, Rachel guessed — instead, the little girl was watching the passengers walking past them. Sitting alone among strangers, it was the reassurance of her brother's voice that was important, and Rachel was sure that the boy intuitively understood this.

The flight attendants began counting passengers, checking seat belts, and closing overhead storage bins. The boy adjusted his sister's seat belt so that it would fit, but let her click the belt together. A caretaker, Rachel thought. *In loco parentis*. In place of parent.

"Do you have our tickets?" the little girl asked her brother.

"Yes."

"Are you sure?"

The boy reached forward, pulled his knapsack onto his lap, and showed his sister the tickets sticking out of a side pocket. "Don't worry, they won't throw us off. He said that just to scare us."

"Are you sure?"

"I'm sure." He put a finger under each eyebrow and raised them, then rolled his eyes down until only the white of each eye showed. "Would I lie to you?" he asked. His sister laughed.

The distraction game, Rachel thought. He already knew how to play it.

A loudspeaker hummed overhead and the pre-flight announcements began as the plane rolled back from the gate and headed out to the runway. A lull in the morning air traffic resulted in almost immediate clearance for takeoff. Engines roaring, the plane accelerated, lifted off, and began its climb.

Rachel looked to her right, where Clare remained immersed in her encyclopedia. The similarities between mother and daughter were unmistakable, Rachel thought, same hair, same eyes, same smile, and, by a quirk of fate, the same birth date — May 14. Tomorrow, Clare would turn 16 and Rachel 41. They took turns deciding how to spend their annual shared day, and this year, because odd-numbered years were Clare's choice, they were going to Los Angeles. For a girl who loved the movies, three days of studio tours, seeing movie sets, learning about special effects, and keeping a lookout for movie stars was the perfect birthday.

Rachel understood her daughter's attraction to films; it was logical. And yet she hadn't been surprised when she overheard a friend of Clare's ask, "Wouldn't you love to be a famous actress?" And beautiful Clare, horrified, had replied, "Never!" She had been spared the actor's appetite for anonymous affection, the "look-at-me" need to be on-stage. But Clare could talk about genres, dialogue, and camera angles as if she'd grown up in Beverly Hills instead of Boulder, Colorado.

Clare was making the teenage years look easy, Rachel thought. In place of the usual anxieties, there was humor and enthusiasm. Rachel was enjoying her daughter's transition from girl to woman.

During the past year, Clare's thoughts and observations had deepened. Without the usual teenager's self-absorption, she was able to look outside herself. Sorting through the words and actions of the people around her, Clare would piece together personalities, characters, and motives. "Sometimes it all fits together," she said. And despite her age, her perceptions were often acute.

The plane leveled off at its cruising altitude and Rachel glanced across the aisle, where the engines' heavy droning had already done its trick: Brother and sister were lost in the heavy sleep of children, her head resting against his shoulder.

Rachel regarded them for several minutes, then from under the seat in front of her, she pulled out her purse. She unzipped a side compartment and withdrew a small, black-and-white photograph. In the picture, a boy and girl, younger than the two across the aisle, were posed stiffly against a high, white fence. Clare looked up and saw the photo in her mother's hand. She craned her neck to see it better. "Who are they?"

"Your uncle and me."

"No!" Clare peered at the boy and girl who wore bathing suits and wary smiles. The photographer's shadow stretched to their feet.

"That's not you," Clare concluded. "The eyes are too different. That girl looks so angry — like she's mad at everyone."

"It's me, and I was mad at everyone."

"How old were you?"

"Five."

"So Uncle Ron was eight?"

"Right."

"What were you so mad about?"

"Everything, and everyone."

"You've never talked to me about your childhood."

"I know."

"But you must think about it sometimes."

"I do — a lot, in fact."

"Why haven't you told me about it?"

"You were too young."

"And now?"

"Now I think you're old enough."

Rachel took a deep breath, as if she were about to swim a long way underwater. "You know that my parents died when I was 17. And, even though this may sound heartless, I'll tell you the truth — I never cried a tear for them. After the car crash and during the funeral, our friends and neighbors all said how brave I was being. They hadn't a clue."

"A clue to what?"

"Families aren't always what they seem. Guessing what goes on inside someone's family is like standing outside a building and guessing what's taking place inside it. At the core of our family was one simple fact: Our parents never wanted children. Ron and I were accidents — unplanned and unwanted — and our parents never hid that from us."

"But after you were born ..."

"Then we were simply unwelcome. They never hit us, there was no physical abuse, but they just didn't care, and maybe that's worse than being hit. Their lives didn't need us. They were focused on things like houses, cars, and clothes. If a genie had appeared, their first wish would have been that Ron and I would disappear."

"What ..." Clare hesitated, picking her words carefully. "What did that do to the little girl in the picture?"

"She felt their rejection to the bottom of her soul," Rachel answered. "My mother had no interest in being a mother. I never knew what it felt like to be someone's daughter."

"In the picture, you look so mistrustful."

"It's who I was; it's who I was going to be."

"But ... ?"

"But because of him," Rachel pointed to the little boy in the photograph, "I became someone else."

"What did Ron do?"

"You've read about what happens in wars, when children suddenly have no parents? How the oldest one stops being a child and begins taking care of the others?"

"He did that after they died?"

Rachel shook her head. "It would have been too late by then. Ron started just about when that picture was taken. I was getting all twisted up emotionally. Having no affection, no love, will do that to you, and somehow he understood that. What he did was make our parents less important in our lives. He was kind and encouraging, and he protected me from their lack of feeling. I was important to him and that became enough.

"And I was so loyal to him." Rachel smiled. "I used to follow him everywhere, and he never showed that he minded, though he must have. One time, he and another boy went swimming at a lake, and he didn't know I'd trailed after them. He didn't see me until the water was up to my neck. I couldn't swim but I'd have drowned trying to follow him. He was my family, my whole family."

"You were a family of two," Clare said.

"Yes. And, though I didn't know it, our parents had no more love for each other than they did for us. Years later, Ron told me that, at night, when he heard them start fighting downstairs, he'd close my bedroom door so I wouldn't hear them; then he'd sit at the top of the stairs, alone in the dark, listening to their hate. I think that's where he ceased to be a child." Rachel paused and looked at Clare. "When you think of the relationship between you and me, what do you think of?"

"I think of you talking to me all the time," Clare replied. "No matter what we're doing together, making dinner, shopping, whatever, we're always talking. And I remember that every time I was sick, you sat in the big chair next to my bed. And when I was really sick, you slept there. And whenever you got mad at me, you never let me go away without giving me a hug and a kiss."

Rachel nodded. "Your uncle talked to me all the time. Every day, he and I talked about my friends, my teachers, my school. He had a great imagination, and, whenever I was sick, before he went to school, he'd ask me what I wanted to hear a story about. I'd give him three or four things, maybe a flower and a princess and a candle, and, during my whole day in bed, I'd wonder about the story he was going to tell me. I couldn't wait for him to get home. When he did, the story he told me was always better than anything I'd imagined. And, in his stories, good always triumphed over evil, which doesn't always happen in the real world.

"Everything we're supposed to get from our parents, I got from your uncle. He was understanding and sympathetic and patient — far beyond what any child should have to be. I don't know how many times I went to him in tears and came away happy. But I never considered what it was doing to him. He needed comforting and he needed understanding, but I was too young. I didn't know."

"Who did he go to when he needed to be a child?" Clare asked.

"For most of his growing up, there was no one there for him. An old couple lived next door until Ron was about six, and he told me that he spent a lot of time at their house. Somewhere, he learned how to be kind — you have to learn it from someone, and I think it must have been from them. I needed him, emotionally, for everything, but he never got to be a boy, or even just a brother; he had to be my mother and father instead."

"He never had a childhood," Clare said. "I can't imagine what that must have done to him."

Rachel nodded. "And you can't skip any stage in life.

Eventually, you have to go back to the one you missed."

"And that's why he ... "

"... went back into his childhood," Rachel said, completing the thought. "That's how he escaped. He saved me and then he tried to save himself, to fix the damage. Ron needed a world he could control, so he surrounded himself with people who don't really exist. Now, they do what he wants, and it makes him happy."

Clare sat back, reconfiguring her perceptions of her uncle. Finally, she looked back at her mother. "It all makes sense."

Mother and daughter, lost in their own thoughts, talked little during the rest of the flight, though Rachel often looked over at the sleeping children, who did not stir until the plane's wheels hit the tarmac at Los Angeles International.

When the aircraft arrived at the terminal, a flight attendant maneuvered between the passengers lining up in the aisle and told the children to wait, saying that she would get off with them. When she returned, she helped them with their knapsacks and accompanied them off the plane, a few passengers ahead of Rachel and Clare, who were still inside the jetway when they heard the shouts of "Mommy!" They stepped out to see a slender woman with auburn hair hugging the children.

The little girl leaned back from her mother's embrace. "Daddy says we have to tell you that we behaved badly all week."

"Oh?" The woman, taken aback by her daughter's honest admission, grinned. "Well, you are wicked children. Did he say how I should punish you?"

The boy answered, "He said you should make us eat lots of ice cream." He was struggling to keep a straight face.

"Chocolate ice cream," said his sister, sensing an opportunity.

"Okay," their mother sighed in mock resignation, "I guess we've got to do it. But do you promise not to cry while you're being punished?"

"We promise!" they chorused.

Rachel and Clare walked past. "Happy children," Clare said. "And we know why they live in Los Angeles."

"Because he lives in Denver," Rachel answered. "Some people are just born nasty."

Farther down the concourse, more than 30 people were gathered in a circle, several of them holding pens and slips of paper.

"Who do you think that is?" Rachel asked as they walked toward the group.

A woman walking in the opposite direction overheard Rachel's question as she passed them. She flourished a signed piece of paper. "It's Aaron Whitfield! And he's signing autographs!"

Clare glanced at her mother and, clutching her movie encyclopedia, ran ahead to the circle of people. With apologies, she snaked her way to the middle, where the famous director, a genial-looking man in his early 40s, was giving autographs and answering questions. He looked up and noticed the young woman standing before him.

Clare stepped forward, put her arms around Aaron Whitfield, and hugged him.

"Uncle Ron," she said, "thank you for my mother." ♦

The Sketchbook

"I don't get it."

"What don't you get?"

Marian Harris glanced across the airplane's aisle at the father and son sitting in Row 22, Seats A and B. The boy, about 10 years old, had his father's bright-red hair and prominent freckles, and across his lap lay a large, open book.

"Clouds. I don't understand clouds."

"What don't you understand about them?"

"Well, look out the window. If clouds are like wisps of smoke, then how come they don't drift apart instead of sticking together? And if they stick together, how come when a plane flies through them, it doesn't come out with cloud stuck all over it?"

"Aw, come on, Dad, I'm trying to read," the boy sighed.

The father, in Seat A, peered out the oval window. "Just

think if you could reach out, grab a piece of cloud, and take it home! You could keep it in a box in the closet, then take it out and play with it whenever you wanted."

"Dad, clouds can't be pets."

The father turned to his son. "Hmmm, you might be right. And if you kept it, what would you name it? And, John, what if it became tame? Would that mean you couldn't release it back into the wild? Maybe it would get so used to following you to school every day that it wouldn't want to go back to 35,000 feet. And what about the ethical and moral questions?" he wondered aloud, gazing out the window again.

The boy regarded his father for a long moment then shook his head slowly and returned to his book.

Marian had been careful not to give away that she was eavesdropping. She noted that the father was tall and lean, bordering on skinny, his hair was tousled, and his clothes were casual and haphazard. In odd contrast, the boy was neatly dressed with his hair combed. They both wore glasses, but the father's were wire rims while the boy's were more somber, with heavy, black frames.

The impression that they created, Marian thought, was of two people in the wrong bodies, for the father had a child's random curiosity, while the boy was the beleaguered parent.

Marian, if asked what kind of impression she thought she left, would have correctly replied, "Almost none at all." She was a woman who was easily overlooked, and she knew it.

She dressed plainly, avoiding bright colors, her skin was fair, and her brown hair had been cut in the same conservative style for 23 years, ever since college.

She never wore makeup, although, once, when she was in her early 30s, she'd walked into a mall through a department store's cosmetics section and had let herself be talked into being made up. Eye shadow, mascara, blush, and lipstick were skillfully applied by the cosmetics saleswoman, who stepped back and blurted out, "Wow! It doesn't usually make such a difference."

Marian didn't know if that was a compliment, but when she walked through the mall, she was aware of people looking at her. A life-long observer of others, she was now suddenly attractive and an object of attention. Men had never stared at her like this, following her with their eyes no matter where she went, and she didn't know whether to return the looks or avoid them. Finally, she went to the ladies' room and wiped off the makeup, the soap stinging her eyes as she struggled to get rid of the mascara.

She bought eye-makeup remover as she left the mall and, when she arrived home, was glad that her mother had already gone to bed, for the traces of lipstick and makeup would have caused comments for a week. No, at least a month, Marian thought, standing in front of the bathroom mirror. She could imagine her mother's words: "What's that war paint on your face?" "So, how loud were they laughing at the painted lady?" "All the makeup in the world won't help you, my dear."

Marian wondered what her second-graders would have said. They'd probably have been confused for a few minutes, then forgotten about it, she decided. They didn't care what their teacher looked like. They were at a great age, she thought, seven and eight years old, and a perfect age for her. The world had not reached them yet; their talk wasn't dominated by movies, music, and clothes — their world was still their families. And often, during recess or lunch, one of the children would ask to sit in her lap. They were too young to care about hiding their need for affection.

For 23 years, Marian had worked at Winnetka Elementary, north of Chicago. Five weeks ago, on the first day of school, she'd stood in front of her new class and been shaken by three of the young faces. Later, she told herself that she shouldn't have been surprised, children often look like their parents did at the same age. What bothered her, she realized, was that a full generation had now passed through her classroom. Her earliest students had grown up, married, had children, and were now sending them back to Miss Harris, who had not married, who'd never had children, and who went home every night to the house she'd grown up in, who went home to dinner with her mother.

Marian's father had died when she was 20. If he'd lived, maybe she'd have moved out after college, she thought. But her mother had been alone, and so Marian had stayed, though it hadn't been easy. Her mother had always had a sharp tongue and let everyone know who was in charge. Marian didn't fight back; it was better not to. She remembered what happened once when her father had tried. And when her mother had a drink, it brought out an even meaner streak, though the cruel words were forgotten the following day. At least by Marian's mother.

The English call them "spinnies." Marian didn't know whether a woman officially became a spinster at age 30 or 40, but she was certain that she qualified now. And yet she was always thinking about "my children" — that was how she described her second-grade class, who every day gave her a dozen hugs. She wasn't sure what she would have done without those bits of affection, although holding a child was different than holding an adult or having an adult hold you, she thought. But who was she to say? She didn't know what it felt like, what it really felt like, to be held. The closest she'd come had been at a cousin's wedding. One of the groomsmen asked her to dance and, as she wavered, he pulled her onto the dance floor. The music was slow, and he talked to her all during the song, but she didn't remember a word he said, for she was overwhelmed by the sensation of his arm around her, of the touching, of his face just inches from hers. She could have kissed him by simply raising her chin. When the music stopped, he walked Marian back to her table, said thank you, and left. And she sat there, suddenly aware of her skin and her breathing as she watched the couples on the floor. She wished the man would come back — and was scared to death that he would.

Marian looked at her watch. The flight had another half-hour before arriving in Chicago. It would continue on to Los Angeles, but she would be back in Winnetka long before it reached California.

California. Marian repeated the word to herself and thought of all the images she'd seen on television. It must be amazing out there, she thought, impulsively wondering what would happen if she "slept" through the Chicago stop. She pictured a flight attendant, somewhere over Colorado, shaking her, and Marian "waking up," trying to act surprised. "Oh, my gosh!" she imagined herself saying. "This is terrible! What should I do?"

She knew what she'd do — rent a convertible, put the top down, and drive through Los Angeles, then go out to the ocean. What was the name of that road, she wondered. The Pacific Coast Highway, she answered herself. Yes, I'd drive on that for a long time, then stop to watch the sunset on the Pacific Ocean ... Marian stopped the images. She could imagine her telephone call home: "Mother, I'm in California. I fell asleep and missed the stop in Chicago." She could imagine the reply: "Marian, sometimes you are the stupidest girl! Everybody must be laughing at you!"

Marian cringed. Whenever she'd had an idea or an impulse and spoken without thinking, her mother's words, sober or slurred, were predictable: "Go ahead — if you want people laughing at you."

Marian had learned not to bring up certain subjects. That's why she never talked about her drawing — she couldn't take the ridicule. When she was young, while both her parents were at work, she'd come home from school and sit in front of the television, watching the afternoon cartoons and idly drawing pictures. One day, she tried drawing a cartoon character. At first, the body was too short, so she lengthened it. The hands were wrong and she didn't know why; then she realized that five fingers on a hand made the character too human, so she changed it to four. She moved the eyes lower in the face — too threatening, she decided, and raised them slightly — good, much happier, even a little silly. And as she drew, she said to herself, "I can do this."

And that's what she did each afternoon. Sitting on the living-room floor, the television on but the volume off, Marian drew the cartoon characters again and again, perfecting their gestures, expressions, and proportions and working out all the mechanics of motion. She learned how one line could make the difference between a bully and a coward, how to mix human anatomy with animal features, and how to make a cat land lightly and a man land hard.

Along the edges of her sketchbooks, Marian drew small, detailed cartoons, then flipped the pages and watched her characters come alive. She learned how to sequence their movements in chases and sword fights, and how to time reactions and expressions. And when each sketchbook was filled, she threw it away so it wouldn't be found.

In high school and college, Marian took art classes, lying to her mother that they were necessary for her teacher's certificate. And because she had talent, she always improved. She now drew pictures for her "children," often as rewards for good work, using her students as her subjects. And parents always wanted to know why, if she drew so well, did she remain a teacher.

"John, do you think this plane has an elevator?"

Marian glanced across the aisle. The boy, without looking up from his book, replied, "Planes don't have elevators. And they don't have escalators either."

"I don't believe it. I'm going to go make sure," the father said. He stood and, as he slipped past his son, lightly touched the boy's hair with his hand, then he headed down the aisle, toward the back of the plane. John turned in his seat and offered a parent's words to his father: "Don't get in any trouble."

John turned forward again and saw Marian looking at him. "We can't take him anywhere."

"Your father has a remarkable imagination."

"Dad has way too much imagination," John replied. "Nothing with him is ordinary. Mom says he doesn't do things like regular people."

"He can't be that different."

John rolled his eyes. "Once a week, Dad cooks dinner, but it's always got a theme. Sometimes it's easy to figure out:

Last week was one of his alphabet meals — we had peas, potatoes, pork, and peach pie. Another night, it was baby onions, brussels sprouts, and meatballs." John looked at Marian, who visualized the meal and laughed.

"That was Dad's 'All-Round' dinner," John said. "You could roll your whole dinner around your plate. And then there was his 'All-Action' meal: duck, squash, waffles, tossed salad, and turnovers."

"He sounds like a great father."

"All my friends think he's the best, but we can't give him anything to do around the house. The other day, Mom asked him to hang a picture while we went to the store. When we got home, the picture wasn't up but Dad had done 20 sketches of a character putting a picture on the wall."

Marian stopped breathing.

"What kind of work does he do?" she asked. She knew the answer. She almost said it along with John.

"He's an animator. He draws cartoons."

"That must be a wonderful job." She heard the words coming out of herself.

"It's perfect for him. I don't know what he'd do if he weren't drawing. I think he'd be pretty miserable. Anyway, Dad and Uncle Harry own a studio. They have about 50 cartoonists who work for them, doing short cartoons, movies, commercials, everything. Dad does all the imagination stuff and Uncle Harry does all the business stuff."

John reached forward and, from a small knapsack in front

of his father's seat, withdrew a sketchbook with the name "David Awtrey" on the cover. He began flipping through the pages. "Dad carries this with him all the time." The first half of the book was filled with drawings of eyes, faces, and a half-dozen noses, and of torsos leaning forward and back, as if they were trying to get their balance.

"I don't know how all this stuff makes for good cartoons," John said. "It's so different. And I really don't understand why he keeps taking anatomy classes. Dad asked me once if I wanted to go with him to a lab and see what an arm looked like without the skin on it." John grimaced. "I told him 'No way.' Once, at Thanksgiving, he started explaining about the turkey's white meat and dark meat. Mom told him to stop before we all lost our appetites."

"Understanding anatomy is vital for an artist," Marian said, staring at the sketchbook's drawings. "A gesture can take six or 60 muscles, and if you don't know what every muscle's doing, the picture looks wrong. You're only drawing the surface, but you have to understand everything underneath. Michelangelo was the first to figure that out."

She glanced at the boy, who looked confused. "He was a sculptor and a painter who lived in Italy about 500 years ago," she said. John nodded and, recognizing Marian's interest in the sketchbook, handed it across the aisle. "Here. You can look at it. Dad won't mind."

Marian took the book and began going through the drawings. One series of eyes appeared identical, but she could see how David Awtrey had shaped the eyebrows, turning them into facial accent marks. The next several pages showed 20 pairs of hands, each pair rendering a different gesture, in fists, in prayer, clutching, touching, and proving again that hands are second only to eyes in their expressiveness. And then there were the torsos, which looked like a sculptor's preliminary drawings, showing a man's torso turning, twisting tighter and tighter until the tension went from extreme to laughable — and she realized that's what he'd been looking for, the dividing line between reality and cartoon.

From overhead came the captain's announcement that the flight was beginning its approach into Chicago. Marian barely noticed. John unbuckled his seat belt and stood up. "I'd better go get Dad," he explained and headed down the aisle.

Marian was grateful that it took the boy a full 10 minutes to coerce his father back up to Row 22. She had already put the sketchbook back into John's seat when she heard them approaching, the father saying it was incredible that the flight crew kept a miniaturizing ray gun onboard. "That's how they shrink those liquor bottles. I wonder if they ever turn the ray gun onto the passengers," he mused, then looked at John. "You know, come to think of it, you're a little shorter than when we got on this flight ..."

"Dad, sit down."

"Are you feeling any shorter?"

"Yes," John replied, ready to agree to anything. "I'm losing a couple of inches every minute. Please sit down."

His father slid into Seat A. John picked up the sketch-book, sat down in Seat B, and looked across the aisle, but the woman's face was turned away, and he guessed she was asleep.

At Chicago, Marian Harris got off the plane, walked out to the parking lot, got into her car, and drove back to Winnetka. So close, she thought. She could imagine her mother's words. "Marian wants to be a cartoonist! Marian, you are a cartoon! Oh, wait, is that the telephone? Quick, Marian, that might be Hollywood calling!"

Her mother wouldn't be able to laugh at her now, Marian thought as she drove home, but she noticed her fingers were trembling on the steering wheel.

———◆———

David Awtrey looked across the big room at Awful Productions and smiled. Fifty artists were working on draw-ing boards or computers — a scene that gave him deep sat-isfaction. He was a cartoonist first, but there was more to life than just putting pencil to paper, and one of his pleasures was looking out at this room of animators, storyboard artists, inkers, painters, and background artists. Every one of them loved the work, he thought; it's what they were born to do. Where else could you find 50 employees who all arrived early for work, stayed late, and laughed often?

David turned in his artist's chair and looked at the sketch hanging on the wall behind him. Six weeks ago, he'd found it on the last page of his sketchbook. It was perfectly crafted, drawn fast but well. The picture showed himself and John as he knew they really were — the boy in a man's body and the man in a boy's body. They were shown side by side in an airplane, David holding a cloud in his hand and John looking at him in disbelief.

But it was the lower right corner of the page that David had spent a long time studying; it was this corner that bothered him so much, for there was nothing there now, just the faint impression of letters and numbers. He had tried using a magnifying glass, tracing paper, then a pencil rubbed sideways as he attempted to decipher what had been there, but all he knew was that a name and a telephone number had been written, then erased.

He remembered the sketchbook being out on the flight back to California, and, when he asked John, he learned about the woman across the aisle. David did not remember her, she'd left no impression, but he could imagine the impulse she must have had, taking a pencil and making this sketch that would eventually be found with her name and telephone number down in the corner. And then she must have felt suddenly foolish and used the eraser. But, he noted, she hadn't torn the page out — she was proud of her work.

David looked at the sketch on the wall. He didn't believe

in coincidence. She should be here. He would have hired her on the spot. The talent was there; you could see it in a second, he thought. That's the way it was with the good ones.

David Awtrey shook his head, turned his back on the sketch, and returned to the work he loved. ♦

Last Flight From Moscow

"Welcome aboard, General Bukharin."

The young woman's Russian accent was nearly flawless, betrayed only by a hint of the South of her native United States. "It's a pleasure to see you again."

The general smiled at the dark-haired flight attendant. "You have been practicing, Grace. Now you sound like you grew up in our Georgia instead of your own."

"Thank you, general."

For three years, General Gregori Bukharin had been a regular passenger on the Moscow-Frankfurt flight. Grace looked at his ticket, then glanced at him.

"You're not in first class tonight?"

"No, my plans changed. I need to get to Germany a few days sooner."

"If someone doesn't show, I'll move you up to first

class," she promised.

"Thank you, Grace."

Bukharin walked back to Row 22, which was empty. He took off his winter overcoat and the wide, blue-gray general's hat, and put them into the overhead storage bin. Stay calm, he told himself.

The general settled into his seat, gave Grace a nod of thanks, then leaned back and closed his eyes. She studied his face with its strong Slavic features — he was in his 50s, she guessed, and a handsome man, the kind who made a woman feel very feminine just by the way he smiled at her.

She'd read his name in the newspapers and knew that he was in the Defense Ministry, and she also knew that he wasn't like the other military officers on her flights; he didn't need stiff drinks or scared attachés to make himself feel important. Bukharin's specialty was negotiation, and he must be good at it, she thought — and even better at the Kremlin's intrigues to have survived since Brezhnev.

Bukharin usually asked Grace about her sisters, and she had been practicing a story about them, in Russian, of course, but this evening he did not ask. Even with his eyes closed, there was weariness and tension in his face. Grace walked back to Row 22, took a pillow from the overhead bin, laid it on the seat next to him, and, as she moved away, decided to take especially good care of the general on this flight.

The plane was big, the boarding was slow, and General

Gregori Bukharin could feel the sweat running down his chest and sides. He opened his eyes and checked his watch — 21 minutes to takeoff, 21 damned minutes, he thought, come on, come on! He remembered the clock atop St. Petersburg's Lenin Museum, its hands motionless for more than 60 years, frozen to the moment of Lenin's death. Even Father Time wasn't safe from this absurd system, he thought.

This is what it felt like to be a child, Bukharin recalled. Every minute lasts an hour when you're young, you've done something wrong, and are dreading discovery. He glanced again at his watch — seven seconds had passed. Bukharin imagined that he could hear each slow tick. Who was that American writer, he asked himself, the madman who wrote about madmen? Poe! Yes, Poe would have liked this, Bukharin thought. Will the traitor live, or will the traitor die?

Pretend it will be two hours until takeoff, he told himself; let the time come to you. He closed his eyes and tried to move his thoughts away from the plane. He retraced his route through the terminal at Sheremetyevo, back along Leningradskiy prospekt, and into Moscow. No, thought Bukharin, the trip did not start there, today; it began 17 years ago at a small table where a conversation could not be overheard.

19 March 1973 / "Colonel Bukharin," said the white-haired man with the calm voice, "we know that you were approached by the Germans, the British, and the CIA. And we know that you turned each of them down and reported their recruiting attempts to the KGB. Please, why are you willing to work with us?"

The colonel looked at the old Russian and then at the silent American sitting with them, who had not introduced himself to Bukharin.

"The KGB has a film they show to new recruits," replied Bukharin. "It's of a traitor being lowered, slowly, into a blast furnace. His screams are like nothing you've ever heard. And I remember when Penkovsky was executed for telling the Americans how far Khrushchev would bluff in '62. The KGB has informants and microphones in the CIA's Moscow station, at SIS headquarters in London, at the BND in Munich. Eventually, someone would get drunk and careless and a name would be mentioned. And if that name was ever 'Bukharin,' the furnace would be stoked again."

"But you think we are different," said the old Russian.

"For five years, intelligence has been reaching Washington about Soviet satellites, spies, weapons development, and troop movements. It's coming out of several ministries, not just the Red Army or Internal Affairs. It isn't just one mole with the highest clearance; it is a network, and it is very, very well run. There have been no whispers, no leads, no threads for the KGB or GRU to follow."

"But you found us, Bukharin," said the old man.

"In each ministry, a different group of people had access

to the stolen information. Like the KGB and GRU, I, too, checked for the existence of a common acquaintance, an old school or military post, or a shared habit. There was none. But there is an outlawed organization, one that is not in dossiers, one that the computers don't follow, and there I found the link: the Russian Orthodox Church. I discovered that certain people in each ministry had a friend or relative imprisoned for religious activities. The pattern wasn't pure, but it was enough. The Church was their motive, and it became their means."

Bukharin studied the white-haired man for a moment. "Each spy had contact with a local priest, and every priest had contact with you. The Church was the perfect conduit for spies against the system. You, Patriarch, would work against a government that claims there is no God."

"Bukharin, you are as smart as we have been told," said the patriarch. "That explains your rise at the ministry. But why are you willing to turn against your motherland?"

"I'm not. The state is not Mother Russia. I believed in the communist ideals when I came into the army. When I was 18 and I put on a soldier's cap for the first time, I was proud of it. That pilotka meant a lot to me. But then I served in Czechoslovakia, Poland, and Hungary, and I felt like a fool for having been so naive. I did not know that my education was just propaganda. I saw battalion commanders preach Lenin's ideals to their troops, then sell their soldiers' food and ammunition. Mother Russia never had a chance. We had

300 years of tsars, ignorance, and poverty; then Lenin, Trotsky, and communism took over. All we did was exchange tyrannies. We are patriots looking for a government to be loyal to.

"I was stationed in Western Europe twice, and I've seen for myself what 'free' looks like. The people there don't need a bottle of Stolichnaya every night to be happy. I want to give Russia a chance, and that will not happen until this government is gone."

The priest looked at the American, who understood that this was his cue.

"My name is Cantrell, and my job is to get information out of the USSR. I am the person who worries about security. It is our first priority. Only the Patriarch and I know the names of all our agents. None of you will ever be told another's identity unless it's an emergency. Neither Pentothal nor torture can make you reveal what you don't know.

"The CIA and SIS handle the week-to-week information. We don't want a steady flow of product — that would be too easy to trace, and eventually it would point back to you. We only want a few big hits, maybe once or twice a year."

"And how would I contact you?" asked Bukharin.

"We will give you a telephone number in Moscow to call. No one will answer — that way the call can't be traced. Call twice, letting the phone ring once each time. We will meet you immediately."

The three men sat in silence for nearly five minutes as Bukharin considered their words; then he nodded.

"Yes."

1 May 1975 / Colonel Bukharin had been assigned to the Kremlin, where he often worked late, even on the May Day holiday. It was evening, and the military parades were long since finished. He flicked off the office lights, walked down the corridor, and waited for an elevator. One arrived, he stepped in and pushed a button as the doors closed.

A hand sliced between the doors, which shuddered and reopened. A tall man with brown, almost simian eyes and wearing a black fur hat stepped in. "Good evening, Colonel Bukharin. You are working late."

"And so is the KGB, Colonel Radek," Bukharin replied as the doors closed again.

"Many people wish we did not work such long hours," said Radek, a mock hurt in his voice. "But, you know, Bukharin, I love my work. I think I have the best job in Moscow, perhaps all of Russia. It is a great game, this hunting of spies. Some of them I track down; others I trap. Some are big; some are little. A spycatcher never knows what he will catch — it might be young or old, male or female, American, European, or even Russian. Some are scared; some are brave."

Radek regarded Bukharin for a long moment.

"Now, you, Gregori Bukharin, I think that you would be

119

a very good spy. You would be brave without being stupid. And you would be hard to catch. But, you know, sometimes a spy has no luck, like a bear that avoids the traps and the hunters, but then it breaks a leg and, lying in the snow, knows that the wolves will find it."

The elevator slowed, came to a halt, and the doors opened. Radek stepped out, then turned and looked back at Bukharin. "I'm glad that no such thing will ever happen to a patriot like yourself, comrade. Good evening."

7 January 1990 (Christmas Day in Russia) / General Bukharin looked down from his office window at the couples and families taking a Christmas evening walk through Red Square. In homes across the USSR, presents had been quietly exchanged and prayers said in front of small, framed icons, for the day was still held holy. Through the coming year, infants would be secretly baptized, and crosses would appear on graves while everyone proclaimed their belief in a system that they knew didn't work. The real Mother Russia was going to win — it was clear now — and Bukharin could feel it coming. One more revolution, he thought. Maybe we'll get it right this time.

In a few years, Lenin's statues would be gone, the black-marketeers would be explaining capitalism to their friends, and Siberia would be just a cold, distant place again, not a threat. And there would be confusion as everyone tried to squeeze a century into a decade or two. The growing pains would be difficult, but it would have been wonderful to watch, Bukharin thought.

Two months ago, the Germans had stood triumphant atop the Berlin Wall. Cantrell told Bukharin that most of the spy network's members were going to the West, out of the USSR, for it was safer to be out of reach. And Bukharin agreed. In the past 17 years, he had identified a dozen Russian spies, including a British ambassador's wife, he had passed along the specifics of each year's USSR arms production, and revealed the Soviets' military plans for Afghanistan. If he stayed, he would always have reason to worry. In the last weeks, Bukharin had seen each of his friends for a final time, but he never said good-bye. He had traveled too much to have ever established a family, and maybe that was for the best, for he would leave no one behind when, in four days, he took his last flight from Moscow.

Because it was Christmas and a Sunday, the Kremlin's offices were empty, as Bukharin had hoped. This was a good time to get work done — work that did not need any observers.

Bukharin put on his gloves, took a ring of keys from a jacket pocket, and began the process of opening the connecting doors between offices. He could not go out into the hallway where the security cameras waited, and so he went through 12 doors until he reached the one that he wanted.

For six years, whenever General Anatoly Miliukov was away from Moscow, Bukharin would look into Miliukov's safe. He'd never found anything interesting, even the supposedly erotic letters from Miliukov's mistress were dull. But, last week he heard a whisper that Miliukov had been given a very important list of names, which was why Bukharin was making one last visit. Come on, Miliukov, he thought, give me a Christmas present, a going-away present.

Bukharin had the old safe's dual combinations memorized by now. He spun the big dials then grasped the shiny handle, twisted it, and pulled the heavy door open. On the top shelf, as always, were the little pink letters. The second and third shelves were bare, but on the fourth shelf was a brown envelope. The door, weighted to swing shut, rested against Bukharin's knee while he opened the envelope and read down two columns of names and a listing of Eastern European cities — Cracow, Prague, Belgrade, and others. At the bottom was a handwritten order, underlined twice: "Review and Destroy." Generals weren't much good at following orders, thought Bukharin.

He read the names a second time, now certain who they were. It will never stop, he thought. Old spies never die; they just get reassigned. Here were the new aliases and assignments for 20 Soviet spies. Moles being sent underground again.

Bukharin reached inside his coat pocket and pulled out the old, drab-green pilotka with the red piping. The symbol of my innocence, he thought. He'd kept it as a reminder of what he'd believed in, and then it had become a good-luck charm. You do not survive and succeed in the Red Army and as a spy without having some very good luck, that was for sure.

Bukharin tucked the cloth cap into the door of the safe, along the bottom edge, to prevent it from closing. Then he took the list over to Miliukov's desk and began copying it. He was 20 feet from the safe, the small, line-by-line duplicator in his hand, when he heard the click. Bukharin spun around. The heavy door had closed, its weight compressing the cloth hat until one of the tumblers fell into place.

"Oh, no," Bukharin said softly. He tried to spin the dials, but they would not move unless the door was closed and both tumblers had clicked into place. Bukharin swore without making a sound. There was not enough of the pilotka showing to pull on it. Bukharin leaned on the safe door, trying to press it hard enough for the second tumbler to click. It was futile.

Bukharin put the small copier into his pocket, along with the sheet of names and the brown envelope. He relocked the connecting doors and, a few minutes later, walked out of the Kremlin into the gently falling snow. Miliukov would not return to Moscow for two more days, thought Bukharin, I must be gone by then. He weighed the odds of disappearing now, tonight, but a smuggled exit from the USSR would be even more dangerous, especially for a general. When a country is a prison, you do not leave at will. Bukharin walked for a long way that evening; then he found a telephone and dialed a number in Moscow where there was no answer.

8 January 1990 / Fragments of conversation reached Bukharin as he walked down the Kremlin's hallways the following morning. "A paper is missing ... they found a pilotka ... only a few people ... they have a list ... they are sure ... today ..."

At 11 a.m., the doors to the Kremlin were closed; then the hallway extending from Bukharin's office to Miliukov's was sealed off. Guards armed with AKs appeared at each end, and the door to Bukharin's office opened without a knock.

Two more guards, also armed with AKs, entered, followed by Radek, who walked up to Bukharin's desk. The general stood, but, before he could speak, Radek threw the pilotka onto Bukharin's desk.

"What is this?" Bukharin asked contemptuously.

"Put it on," Radek said.

"The KGB should be kept on a leash, Radek. Someday it will bite the wrong person."

"Put it on," Radek said flatly. "This was left by a man who has stolen state secrets."

Bukharin looked down at the cap with its red piping. He picked it up and, as the three men watched, put it on his head. The hat slid down, almost comically, over his forehead.

Bukharin's disbelief never showed. "Too bad, Radek. It's too big," he said, and dropped the cap onto the desk.

Radek stepped forward and snatched up the pilotka. "I am surprised, General Bukharin. I was sure that the traitor was you."

Long after the three men had left, Bukharin remained standing behind his desk, staring at the door.

"Welcome aboard Flight 1739. This is ..."

The pilot's voice startled Bukharin. "We have completed our boarding and are just a few minutes from takeoff. Please make sure your ..." Bukharin could picture Grace pulling the passenger door shut, then twisting the locking bar. Yes, he thought, yes! Through his window, he saw the cowled end of the boarding ramp draw back and swing away. A tractor pushed the plane back, turning its nose out toward the runways.

Flight 1739 taxied across the tarmac and waited as three flights took off; then it moved into position at the head of the long, paved strip. The engines revved higher and higher until only the brakes were holding it back. Release! Bukharin urged, come on! But the revving continued, and continued, and then the turbines' pitch changed and dropped. Flight 1739 rolled slowly down the runway, turned right, and headed back to the terminal. The captain's announcement was brief. "Ladies and gentlemen, we have been called back to the gate."

Bukharin sat motionless. So close, he thought, and now

there was no way out, no escape. This, he told himself, is how the bear feels while it lies in the snow, waiting for the wolves. At the gate, the boarding ramp was extended. Grace twisted the handle and swung the door out. Into the plane stepped a tall man wearing a black fur hat and holding in his right hand a soldier's drab-green pilotka.

Radek stopped and stared at the faces in first class, then he strode down the aisle, looking left and right, past Rows 8, 12, 17, 20, 21. He stopped a few feet from the general, raised the pilotka, threw it at Bukharin's chest, then slumped into the seat next to him.

"Gregori Bukharin," Radek said wearily, "you nearly got us both killed." ♦

Here Tomorrow

C harlie Elliott studied the black cellphone in his hand. For the past hour, he'd been waiting for it to ring, hoping it would, afraid that it would. Midnight had passed, and there was only the hint of a breeze; it was like that in late July, when the heat threaded through the days and the nights.

It was quiet on the rooftop, 12 stories above the streets of Providence, eight stories above the operating room. When the surgery was finished, his phone would ring and the surgeon would tell him the outcome; then Charlie, the hospital's spokesman, would call the newspapers and television stations.

Every story would use the same picture, he was sure. It would show a clear-eyed, dark-haired girl whose smile was about to burst into laughter. Charlie had never seen her like that, for it was an old photograph, taken more than a year ago, when Sarah Pierson was eight, back when she was well.

At Providence Hospital, every administrator was required to spend one day each year walking rounds with doctors and observing surgeries. Charlie remembered the kidney transplant he'd seen and the moment that the new kidney, sewn into place, suddenly came alive, transformed from dull yellow to bright, healthy pink. But he could not watch the operation tonight. He needed to be up here, out in the air, under the stars.

If anyone from the newspaper, anyone he used to work with, had walked onto the roof and seen him, sitting alone, as close to prayer as he'd ever been, they'd have laughed out loud. "Hey, where's the real Charlie Elliott?" he imagined them shouting at him. "Where's the old Charlie?"

"Gone," he would have told them. "Gone forever."

And if they asked what happened, he had an answer, a quote borrowed from somewhere: "If you want to hear the gods laugh, tell them your plans for the future." The gods were laughing now, he thought, laughing loud and long, for they'd let him slide through half a life, 40 years, just to set him up.

Charlie remembered back a dozen years ago, when he was working at the newspaper. A rookie reporter, a young woman, was taking dictation about four children killed when a scaffolding collapsed at their school. She wasn't crying, but her eyes were wet, and when she put down the phone, Charlie told her that if she was going to be a bleed-ing heart on every story she handled, she'd better find another job.

Nothing bothered Charlie Elliott, and everyone in the newsroom knew it. In 25 years at the paper, he must have said "Here today, gone tomorrow" a thousand times, including once at a fire as he was stepping over the bodies. That became part of newsroom legend.

Charlie thought of Sarah Pierson, who lay asleep down-stairs, her body opened up, the transplant team around her. He and she were as dissimilar as two human beings could be, but he recognized a shared fact: To have a new life, they had each needed someone to die.

Charlie met Sarah on the day he was accompanying her doctor during rounds. He remembered her because she was the same age as Molly, and Sarah also had a stack of books next to her bed with many of the same titles: *Black Beauty*, *Harry Potter*, and *The Secret Garden*.

Later, the doctor explained to Charlie that when Sarah was six, she'd had a kidney removed because a tumor had grown inside it. Now, more tumors were growing in her remaining kidney "and it will have to come out, too. She's on the national waiting list, so each time a kidney becomes available, the computer searches the list for the highest-ranking good match. We could get a call in the next five minutes or never get one at all."

Her parents had begged to serve as living donors, but

their compatibility was compromised by hypertension, and Sarah had no siblings. Charlie suggested getting Providence's newspapers and television stations involved "because they're always looking for stories with happy endings — especially if the media played a part in it." An appeal went out, but no match was found, and the stories had taken on grim tones.

Every few days, Charlie would stop by Sarah's room, and he usually found her reading, escaping into her imagination. She liked to hear about Charlie's daughters and what they did and what they liked. He did not bother with empty words of encouragement, because the girl with sallow skin and graying eyes was too wise for that now.

Sarah endured the dialysis, the tests, and the pain with the uncomplaining courage of a child, but Charlie knew it was aging her. She wasn't a nine-year-old anymore, she wasn't like Molly, so impatient with life. One morning, Charlie heard Sarah asking her parents about God and death, and he understood that it wasn't curiosity; she was preparing herself.

Too short a life, Charlie thought, while he'd been given two. The newspaper was the life that Charlie had planned — he was going to be like his father, for Mike Elliott had been, without argument, the best hard-news reporter in Providence and the most popular guy in any bar.

Charlie's mother died before he turned three, so he grew up with just his father. At breakfast, Mike would give

Charlie a nickel for every mistake he found in the newspaper, and that's how Charlie earned his allowance, finding misspellings, typos, wrong names, and botched facts. Mike claimed that by the time Charlie was 10, he was better than half the editors on the copy desk, and by the time he was 16, he was better than the other half.

While Charlie was in high school, he pulled weekend shifts at the paper, either desking or reporting. He didn't bother with college. For eight years, Mike and Charlie had all the city's best stories, but then Mike's liver gave out. He was only 54, but, as Eddie Reed, one of the longtime editors, said in a eulogy, "He had a helluva run, and what was wrong with that?"

Charlie continued on, learning the city's politics, its history, and its characters. He was a great storyteller, whether he was sitting at a keyboard or leaning on a bar. And if an attractive woman was present, he knew how to play the role of the hard-drinking reporter, with a touch of the rogue thrown in.

When he reached 40, Charlie was right on course — he was the best reporter in the city, and a local magazine named him "Best Guide for a Pub Crawl." The accompanying photo showed a stocky man standing outside a bar with his shirtsleeves rolled up and a drink in one hand. He had reddish-brown hair and a challenging look that hadn't lost its humor.

Charlie's life was simple and familiar: up by 10 a.m.,

breakfast at a diner before the lunchtime crowd came in, then to work. He'd make the rounds, talking to anyone and everyone, listening for a tip, a rumor, or a joke with some truth hidden inside it. Twice, Charlie was offered a columnist's job, and he turned it down both times. "I write news, not opinions," he said. "And I like it out on the front page."

Dinner in the newsroom was always takeout, and Charlie ate while he finished his stories. After the first edition was put to bed, someone would announce, "Let's go, we deserve one tonight," and Charlie would join the group that headed across the street to The Deadline, the bar where the reporters repeated the stories they'd just written.

Charlie was comfortable in a bar. He liked the laughter, the noise, and the feel of a glass in his hand. And he always knew what to do and what to say. One of the old sportswriters said with approval that watching Charlie walk into a bar was like watching Ted Williams come up to the plate. "He was a natural."

Like his father, Charlie loved the booze — the taste of it, the smell of it, and the high. He didn't drink in the morning, "Never before breakfast," and only pride stopped him from drinking on the job. Maybe that's what saved him, he realized later. Each night, Charlie drank until The Deadline closed, then walked the three blocks to his apartment, "just within staggering distance," and never remembered falling asleep.

Charlie was in the newsroom on the Friday night that Jack

Watson, a sportswriter in his mid-30s, came in and announced that his wife, Tina, had just given birth to their second child, another girl. Jack went out to celebrate and never made it home.

For six weeks after the funeral, the newsroom staff took turns stopping by the Watson house to run errands, do yard work, and lend a hand. The reporters and editors gradually went back to their normal lives — only Charlie kept showing up.

On a weekend afternoon in November, he came to rake leaves and, as often happened, was invited to stay for dinner. Afterward, while he was talking to Tina, three-year-old Molly climbed into his lap, curled up, and, without a word, went to sleep. Nothing like that had ever happened to Charlie Elliott.

During the next months, he read nursery rhymes that he'd never heard before; checked in closets and under beds for monsters; and had long, serious discussions about vegetables.

One night, after the girls were in bed, Tina asked Charlie, "Were you ever a kid?"

"What?"

"You know, a kid, one of those short people who runs around talking about Santa Claus and the Tooth Fairy."

Charlie grinned. "Not really."

"So, you've never put a stocking up over a fireplace or buried your dead goldfish out in the backyard?"

He shook his head. "No fireplace, no goldfish, no back-yard."

"And all this family stuff, the bedtime stories and the kisses good night, it's all strange to you, isn't it?"

"No more than life in any other foreign country."

"Wow," Tina laughed, and for the first time, Charlie Elliott saw the happy woman with whom Jack Watson had fallen in love. And he did, too.

Charlie liked the reporter's life, but every time the little girls kissed him good-bye, it rocked him. A year after Jack's death, Charlie had arrived at a choice, and he knew it. He never went to the Watsons' with liquor on his breath, but he always stopped for a drink on the way home. And he understood that if he wanted to join their lives, there could be no chance of another phone call after another drunk's car wreck.

People always stay in character, no matter what they do, so Charlie quit drinking the way a loner would, the way most people fail. Charlie squeezed his drinking time by staying at the paper a little longer each night and getting to the bar a little later. He didn't know which he missed more, the booze or the bar itself, but the call of "We deserve one" was always tempting, and he finally realized that he couldn't leave the bars without leaving the news-paper, too.

Tina never mentioned his drinking, but she knew his rep-utation. And when Charlie took the PR/spokesman's job at

Providence Hospital, she knew what it meant. She asked what his hours would be.

"Nine to five, generally."

Her reaction was a long, theatrical pause. "Is this going to ruin my budget for weeknight dinners?"

"Probably," Charlie confirmed, and they married a few months later. He hadn't had a drink since, and he didn't have the craving anymore; he'd been one of the lucky ones, and he wasn't going to tempt the fates.

Cellphone in hand, Charlie looked up at the stars, clear and bright in the moonless night. A few weeks ago, Molly, nine years old and trying to piece the world together, had just gotten into bed when she asked if the stars were part of heaven.

"They might be," Charlie replied. "I'm not sure."

"Well, I think they are," she said, "because I think that every star is someone who's died and gone to heaven. And one of those stars is my first daddy."

"Molly, I think you're exactly right," Charlie said. Then he kissed her and six-year-old Melissa goodnight, walked downstairs, went outside, and spent a long time looking up at the night sky.

A few days later, when Charlie stopped to visit with Sarah Pierson, she asked him where heaven was. He gave her Molly's answer.

"So when I die, I'll become a star?" she asked.

"Molly says so."

"Then maybe it won't be so bad," she replied.

She was dying, and she knew it. Her body was poisoning itself and it could not stop. Outside Sarah's room, Charlie often saw her parents in the hallway, trying to maintain their strength, but the wait for a transplant, with its cycle of hope, disappointment, and despair, was grinding them down.

"People die every minute," her father said. "Do they think they're taking their bodies with them? They aren't going to give a kidney ... no, of course not, but I bet they'd be damn glad to get one if they needed it!"

Sarah's energy kept fading. Now when Charlie visited, she was not reading, though a book was always under her hand, unread but still reassuring. He was scheduled to attend a conference in Baltimore, and, when he went to say that he wouldn't see her for a week, she gave him a last request. Charlie told Sarah's doctors, who agreed to tell her parents.

He didn't sleep well in Baltimore, for he kept waking up with the same thought: People know when an illness has won, they know when they're going to die, and before he left the hospital, Sarah Pierson had said good-bye.

Charlie was waiting for the final call, and at 3 p.m. on his last day in Baltimore, his cellphone rang. He stood up from the conference table, walked out into the hallway, and pressed the power button.

"Hello." He dreaded the next words.

"Charlie, we have a donor for Sarah. She'll have the

operation tonight."

"I'll get the next plane back. When will the kidney get there?"

"When you do, Charlie. You're bringing it. The kidney's in Baltimore."

In 20 minutes, he was at Baltimore City Hospital, talking to the head of the organ-recovery team. "The national computer gave us the name of a girl at your hospital. It should be a good match," she said, "but the kidney's not ready yet."

"What's the situation?"

"A 14-year-old kid took his brother's motorcycle but didn't bother with the helmet. A truck hit him as he went through a stoplight. His parents have consented to donate his organs, but his father isn't here yet, so we're keeping the boy on life support."

An hour passed until the boy's father arrived, and then he needed time to say good-bye. He sat alone with his son and cried, and after he left, the ventilator was removed. Within 20 minutes, the transplant team had the kidney out and packed in ice for the trip north.

Charlie was the last passenger to board the 6:45 flight to Providence. He was in Row 22, Seat A, with the red-and-white plastic box in the seat next to him, the safety belt looped through its handle and pulled tight. Charlie laid his jacket over the cooler.

At T.F. Green Airport, in Rhode Island, an off-duty ambulance driver met Charlie; the surgical team was ready and waiting at Providence Hospital.

After they rushed away with the box, Charlie walked up to Sarah's room, where he found her parents sitting in silence.

"She has a chance now," he said, and they nodded without speaking. They had no words left. Sarah's father reached into his pocket, pulled out an envelope, and gave it to Charlie, who, as he walked out of the room, wondered how he would have felt waiting for the outcome of an operation on Molly or Melissa. If someone had come into the room and said, "Here today, gone tomorrow," Charlie would have punched him in the mouth.

Standing on the roof, the stars above him, Charlie withdrew the envelope from his pocket, opened it, and pulled out the signed form letter, authorizing Providence Hospital and its doctors to take all usable organs and tissue from the body of Sarah Pierson. Her parents' approval was enough, but another signature was on the page, written in the large, unsteady letters of a child.

Charlie flinched at the sound of the cellphone. He hit the power button. The voice on the other end belonged to the head of the transplant team. When she finished, Charlie thanked her, turned off the phone, and looked up at the stars for a long moment before punching in a new number.

"Copy desk, Reed speaking."

"Eddie, it's Charlie. Sarah Pierson was operated on tonight."

"Oh, hell, everyone's across the street. All I've got here are a couple of rookies who can't write. Charlie, could you dictate a story to one of them?"

"Sure."

There were two clicks; then a young voice came on the line. "I'm ready."

"Okay, here we go," Charlie said, and he could feel the wetness in his eyes. "Sarah Pierson's final wish will have to wait for another day. The nine-year-old girl dying of kidney failure wanted her organs donated for transplant. Last night, she underwent surgery to receive a kidney — it was a perfect match." ♦

A Promise to Eddie Gray

I am an honest man. I do not lie to my friends; I do not lie to my enemies; I do not lie to myself.

But every day I look into people's eyes and tell them what isn't true, and that is how I make my living.

I am an actor, an honest actor. Sounds like a contradiction, doesn't it? But it is true, and it is by choice, for no one is honest by chance. You make that decision once; then you affirm it a thousand times, or maybe a million.

I can make you cry with stories of a childhood I did not have, inspire you with dreams I never had, and tell you secrets I do not have, and you will believe my every word. But I will only do it on a stage or for a camera. For 26 years, I've kept a promise, a promise made to my 10-year-old self, and I will not let that boy down.

"Welcome aboard Flight 213 from Los Angeles to New York, then continuing on to Rome, Italy ..."

Los Angeles, New York, Rome — they are all a long way from central Florida.

I now think of Eddie Gray as if he were someone else, for I am in awe of him. The child is the father of the man, and I owe more to that boy than to anyone I'll ever meet. I don't know how he did it, but he did not give in; he did not yield. Instead, piece by piece, he built himself, and what he invented was me.

"Ladies and gentlemen, we ask that you ..."

In my pocket, next to my ticket, is a second ticket, unused, unoffered. And in that same pocket is a small, velvet-lined box with a ring in it, unused, unoffered.

The filming will begin in a week, just north of Rome. This is my 15th movie, and the 12th to go on location. There is a strange, vagabond energy to location work. Like 200 gypsies, we gather for a few months, an instant community with one unifying purpose. There are fights, affairs, jealousies, and camaraderie, and, when the shooting is done, there is a party.

On the following day, the family breaks up, never to gather again.

This time, the location shooting was going to be different for me. It was going to start with an introduction of Lora to the cast and crew. She would have blushed, and when the calls came "Let's see the ring!" she'd have held out her left hand and waved her fingers, letting the diamond catch the light, and she'd have smiled that beautiful smile.

It is hard to look at the empty seat next to me, Seat B of

Row 22, for I'd imagined this flight a hundred times; you do that when you love someone. I'd pictured the words and the touches, and falling asleep against each other. People we love become so familiar to us that we do not need to summon their image from memory, for they are always before us. Her blue eyes and black hair, offset by fair skin, are what draw people to her; her wit and warmth are what holds them.

Here, on the plane, every passenger would have noticed her, and some would have recognized her from the films she's made. And what about me? I would have been looked at only because I was with her. I do not have a leading-man's face, one that is more handsome than interesting, and that is my good fortune. Instead, I look like anyone — a soldier, a senator, a psychopath — anyone. And in every movie contract, I stipulate that I will not wear a beard or glasses in the film because it is with them I pass unnoticed through life. Stars seek the luxury of isolation, but actors need people, for that is where we find the accents, gestures, and mannerisms that we need.

Olivier said that his three reasons for acting were: "Look at me. Look at me. Look at me." I, too, had three reasons: "Get out. Get away. Get free."

Last March, after the Academy Awards, a magazine sent a reporter and a photographer down to central Florida, to the town of Corey, where they found my brother and a few of the neighbors who'd never moved away. The photographer was good at his job — he knew where to be at 3:23 a.m. The photo shows a wall of rushing train passing behind a rusting metal box of a mobile home; the 60 feet between house and tracks were shortened to inches by the photographer's lens.

I remember how that box shook at 3:23. I always woke up, and our father did, too. A few minutes later, he would get Jack and me out of bed and drive us to one of the big orange groves. As our father slept in the car, Jack and I worked as moonlighters, picking the best oranges, the ones high on the outside of the trees' south side, while the orange blossoms perfumed the night air with their heavy, sweet scent.

We'd go home and sleep for a few hours, then Jack and I would go off to school while our father headed west, toward Port Charlotte, to find a shady spot next to a busy road. He'd pull out the "Fresh Fruit" sign that he'd stolen up in Georgia, prop up the boxes of oranges in the trunk, and sit in a lawn chair, listening to the radio, a beer in his hand. And he'd boast to every customer, "I got life beat."

On rainy days, Jack and I weren't allowed to go to school; instead, our mother took us to the supermarkets. She'd buy a few big, cheap items, like soda and chips, while Jack and I stole everything else, especially meat, cheese, and anything imported, hiding them in the large, lined pockets she'd sewn inside our overcoats. If the rain lasted all day, our mother would drive us around to at least a dozen stores, and we never got caught. We learned how to talk to the lady at the checkout counter, asking polite, distracting questions so she'd look at our faces instead of our coats. I learned how to act while I was stealing.

Every night, our parents went down to the Crab Shack to drink, leaving Jack and me in the trailer. After they were gone, Jack always headed out, but I stayed because inside our TV was a world unlike anything in Corey, Florida. I saw countries, cities, families, love, and heroes on that TV. I saw people with poise and class who spoke and dressed and moved like no one I'd ever met. Alone in that trailer, I listened to their words and repeated them just the way they'd been said. I noticed that these people didn't slouch against walls or chairs; they didn't talk in edgy, endless streams of taunts, sneers, and boasts; and there was expression in their eyes, whether it was amusement, anger, despair, or something else. I lay on my parents' bed, trying to put those same expressions into my eyes. But, later, when the TV was off and everyone was home, I acted just like them.

In school, I wasn't the class clown or a show-off, I wasn't the most athletic, the smartest, or the one who was everybody's friend, but what I had was the best memory, and I knew I was the most observant. And as I talked to the supermarket cashiers, I realized that I was a good liar.

My parents' lives were full of deception. I can't guess how many times they said: "Don't tell your mother what you just saw ..." and "Don't tell your father what you just heard ..." They lied to one another and cheated on each other, too, sometimes quietly, sometimes blatantly, and I wonder now if they did some of it just out of boredom. I know that's why they swore as much as they did — the obscenities gave their everyday thoughts an added force, as if their words were important. Because I learned how to speak from them, on my first day of school, I was sent home and I didn't understand why.

My mother's brother, Clyde, owned an airboat, and sometimes when he was giving tourists a ride, he'd let me come along. With that big propeller roaring, we skimmed across the swamps, and I imagined I was leaving Corey forever. Afterward, when they'd paid and left, he'd open a beer and we'd sit on his dock and talk. Uncle Clyde told the truth about things. Once, when I was 10, I asked him what he thought of my parents.

He didn't hesitate a second. "They're scum — they'd have to be to turn their own sons into shoplifters and thieves. I'm always surprised when I actually hear one of them tell the truth. I assume it's because they just couldn't think of a lie quick enough.

"And because they lie to everyone, they figure everyone must be lying to them, so they're always suspicious of people. It's a nasty way to go through life, Eddie. But everybody gets to decide who they're going to be. Jack's already decided he's going to be like your parents. He can't imagine anything else."

"So what's going to happen to me?" I asked, suddenly

feeling like I was talking to a fortune-teller.
"It's your choice, Eddie." He took a long drink. I waited.
"But I'll tell you what I think. I think you're going to come
out of this fine because you're trying to figure out the difference between right and wrong. If there was still a church
in Corey, I think you'd have probably snuck in and asked the
minister a month's worth of questions. But there isn't a
church and there isn't a minister, so you're here, getting
Uncle Clyde's version of life.

"You're a good kid, Eddie, you want to do the right thing,
and you'll figure out how to do it. So, what I'm telling you
is that I've got faith in you. You're going to be OK."

I held on to those words like they were gold. For the
next eight years, I know I thought about them every day,
because everybody needs someone to believe in them, and
all it takes is one.

For those eight years, I sorted through people's traits and
habits, picking out the ones I wanted for myself and remem-
bering the rest for characters. I understood what honesty felt
like, how much it means when someone trusts you, and I felt
what forgiveness does for the giver, because Uncle Clyde
had warned me not to be bitter about what my parents had
tried to make me. "Just leave it behind," he said. "Don't poison your soul over them."

My parents never asked what I wanted to be when I grew
up, and I never told them. After high school, I hitchhiked to
New York City and found work in Off-Broadway compa-

nies; small, independent films; and soap operas. I learned how to limp (don't exaggerate it; instead, turn your foot in and try to hide it), how to act drunk (it's the same as being exhausted), and when to say a line of dialogue slowly, so the audience will look at you longer. I understood the difference between "large acting" for the back row (in theaters) and "small acting" for the front row (in TV and the movies).

And my acting kept drawing from my life. While in my early 20s, I recognized the fragility of relationships' beginnings, how a look that lasts an extra half-second can trigger awareness, interest, and hope — how an extra half-second can be the difference between love and nothing.

Acting was my skill, my talent, but I remember thinking what a strange profession it was for a man. We put on costumes and makeup, our hair is combed by people who fawn over us, and then we seek the anonymous affection of an audience of strangers. I remember a show when a group of us, actors all dressed as pirates, was waiting for the director's cue to start fighting before the curtain went up. As we stood in position, gaily costumed, one of the old actors said in disgust, "If our fathers could see us now ..."

The parts got bigger, the money got better, and the reviews were always good. When a studio in L.A. offered me the lead in a thriller, I was ready. The film was a hit and so were the next two, which solidified my fame — and, in Hollywood, fame is power. After that, I could arrange to work with the best directors and the best film editors, but some of the biggest stars said no. Twice — once an actor, once an actress — they backed out of films after I'd signed on. Why, I asked, and they each said the same thing: Ed, you can act circles around me. I know it and you know it. And if I stay in this movie, everyone else will know it, too. Sorry.

I was good at the acting and I was good at the business, which meant the money was beyond belief, so every year I pay a debt — on January 1, a new airboat arrives at Uncle Clyde's dock. Other money goes toward a house for Jack and a monthly "loan" of a few thousand dollars. A man with $45 million can't leave his brother in a mobile home.

Our parents are dead, killed one night while weaving their way back from the Crab Shack, but they lived long enough to see that first hit film. I still have the clipping from the Port Charlotte paper that interviewed them. "Oh, we always knew he'd be an actor," my mother said. "We believed in that boy and encouraged him right from the start. It just shows what happens when a boy comes from a good home and a family that loves him."

I've never tried to forget my parents; I've never wanted to pave over my past. Instead, I accept my memories of them, and my childhood. And in a way, I have no choice, because every time I cut an orange, that heavy, sweet smell takes me back to those years.

I used some of my wealth to build a large and beautiful house atop a cliff in Malibu, overlooking the Pacific Ocean, and the nearest railroad track is 16 miles away. I'd never had a home before, only places that I lived. Here, at last, was a sanctuary, which is one reason I did not have a series of young actresses passing through. And I avoided that easy, endless cycle of pleasure, boredom, and farewell; I didn't want to find out exactly when the self-loathing would set in.

At the start of every film, when I meet the leading lady, an uncertainty is quickly answered — whether the two of us will have that crucial chemistry. With Lora, it was there as soon as we shook hands — that extra half-second — and the camera saw it in every scene we played. The filming took four months, and when it was finished, she moved into my house.

The movie was her third, and we were lucky that her next one was set in L.A., so every day for five months, we woke up next to each other, and I'd never known such happiness. I told her my life and she told me hers, and we lived in a rhythm that few people ever get to share. Being with her, I realized what a solitary life I'd led, and I savored the daily exchange of small kindnesses.

I appreciated her and I admired her, and I understood the ambition that brought her from West Texas to Hollywood. She told me that, in high school, half of her class "was married or engaged by the time we were seniors. My boyfriend proposed to me on graduation night, and I asked him if he ever wanted to see London or Paris or Rome. He answered, 'Why would I ever want to go to those places?' He still doesn't understand why I turned him down, but I wasn't going to live and die in a small town like that."

Lora went to college in Dallas, joined a theater group, and saw the path she wanted. After moving to Los Angeles, she began the rounds of auditions, where producers remember women with talent, beauty, and brains. The roles started coming her way.

Our work meshed smoothly with our lives. She read scripts with me as I looked for the best parts. When she wanted, I read her scenes with her, but she often said that it was intimidating having Edward Gray watch her rehearse, so she often practiced when I was away from the house. Sometimes I'd get back a little early and I could hear her as she worked, honing the inflections, the pacing, and the emphasis, building her character out of the words. Her talent and determination were obvious as she worked to load her lines with the emotion that a scene needs.

Actresses need success to happen quickly. Too soon, the lights and cameras show those first lines around the eyes. My career might last another 30 years, but Lora's could be over within five, when the next wave of young actresses assumed the movies' image of eternal, youthful beauty.

One night, I noted the jade band she sometimes wore on the fourth finger of her left hand. I borrowed a jeweler's sizing cone and made sure the engagement ring would fit. Lora's film wrapped just in time for us to go to Rome together, and so the timing was perfect. One week ago, the

Pacific sunset was running through its full palette when I asked her to go down to the shore.

In my pocket was that small, velvet-lined box, my sweating hand around it. We walked on the rocks that form a jetty that juts out into the sea, and when we reached the end, Lora said, "There's something I want to tell you." She hesitated, then continued, "I've never known anyone like you. I've loved other men before, but this morning I woke up before you, and while you were sleeping, for the first time, I could see in your face what you were like as a boy. I could see the hurt, and the pain, and the drive. And that is why I love you."

I looked out at the sea and could feel the tears in my eyes. For the second time, someone's words of belief in me had changed my life. Now she'd shown me even more of who she was, what she valued, and what I meant to her. For a while, it was hard to talk. I didn't know what to say — and then I did.

I've thought of her words so often: "I've never known anyone like you. I've loved other men before, but this morning, I woke up before you ..." Those words would have meant everything if I hadn't heard her practicing them the week before, honing the inflections, the pacing, the emphasis, over and over until they were perfect for her audience of one. Standing out there on the jetty, I told her what I'd heard. She did not argue, she did not cry, and I'm glad she left that night.

I can manipulate emotion on a stage or for a camera, but elsewhere I am like everyone else, taken along on a ride that none of us can plan or control. Unlike trust, love cannot be switched off. There was a sweetness to those months, and now, when I encounter a towel, a pillowcase, or an otherwise empty closet where the scent of her lingers, I do not mind.

I do not hate her and I am not bitter, for I refuse to poison my soul. So I'll keep the ring and the ticket for a while, as they are reminders of hope and love. And because, you see, Eddie Gray would not give in and, I've promised him, neither will I. ♦

Not
An Option

N ick Markison looked up from his newspaper and elbowed his dozing brother.

"Hey, Sleeping Beauty, look who's on our flight!"

Bobby Markison, still hung over from last night's post-wedding party, opened his eyes and sat up. He glanced at his brother, who pointed across the waiting area of Gate 12 at Chicago O'Hare International Airport.

A man in his early 30s, tanned and fit, with gray eyes and short, dark hair, moved with a straight-shouldered, almost-military erectness as two airline personnel escorted him to the jetway door. Everyone was watching, and several hastily found cameras flashed, but the man made eye contact with no one and the group disappeared into the jetway.

"The guy wins the U.S. Open and three hours later, he

looks bummed out," Bobby said, sliding back down in his seat. "What's with him?"

"I don't know," Nick said. "He was fine yesterday, during that TV interview. Then, today, he gets six birdies in the last nine holes, shoots a 29 in the rain on the back side, and he never cracks a smile.

"It's strange. A guy wins a tournament, and usually he's kissing the trophy and holding it up for everyone to see. Leary handed it back as if it was going to bite him. And he didn't say a word. No speech, no interview, nothing."

"Maybe it's got something to do with what happened to his caddie," Bobby wondered, "the one who died a few weeks ago. I'll tell you, that's got to freak you out — watching someone get hit by lightning."

Boarding was announced for Flight 217, direct to New York then continuing on to London. As the Markisons entered the plane, Bobby leaned into first class and saw the champion sitting alone in the last row, a pillow behind his head, eyes closed.

Nick and Bobby walked back to coach and settled into their seats in Row 22. Nick thumbed through the Sunday newspaper, found the sports section, and pulled it out.

"There's a big feature here on Leary," he said.

"What's it say?"

"Let me see ..." Nick scanned the opening paragraphs, "'the hardest-working man on the tour' ... 'a perfectionist' ... OK, here we go, 'To prepare for a tournament, Leary will play or practice 10 to 12 hours a day. He's been known to hit balls until it's dark and then be back on the practice tee at sunrise.'"

"Wow. You don't expect that from a country-club boy."

Nick read on silently, then shook his head. "He isn't. It says his father was an Army sergeant, real tough, who treated his family as if they were in the military, and they all learned that no excuse was good enough. Their father used to say, 'Failure is not an option.' Leary grew up on a series of Army bases, but there was always a golf course nearby.

"'Every time Leary's father was reassigned, Leary went out to the new course and got a job, usually picking up range balls. His family moved 12 times and Leary stopped thinking of any house as his home. 'Home was a golf course,' he said.'"

Nick continued skimming through the article: "'...because he worked at the courses, he got to play for free' ... 'he played all the time' ... 'When Leary was 17, a college coach heard about the Army brat in Amarillo, Texas, who had a perfect swing and could shoot 64s and 65s' ... 'Leary got a full scholarship and won the national collegiate title three times.

"'During his rookie year on the pro tour, Leary won three tournaments on raw ability and mental toughness, then didn't win again for eight years' ... 'Because he was a perfectionist, Leary's rounds often fell apart after his first bad shot. He eventually lost his tour card and played in Europe for a year before getting back on the U.S. tour.'"

Nick looked up. "It doesn't say it here, but I think that was three years ago, about the time he hired the old guy to be his caddie." Nick resumed reading, "'Last year, Leary won four tournaments and $3.1 million.'" He paused. "Nice year."

"Nice life," Bobby said. "What did the caddie have to do with it? Was he a hypnotist, a swing guru, or what?"

"I don't know." Nick scanned the rest of the article. "It doesn't say."

"Where were they when the lightning struck?"

"On a course near Philadelphia," Nick folded the sports section and slid it into the seat pocket in front of him. "It was a Monday and they were practicing when this freak storm came up and the caddie got hit. Leary skipped the next couple of tournaments and went to Scotland for the funeral, but he played again the next week, did OK, and he won the Open today, so I guess it didn't bother him that much."

Bobby was silent for a while; then he said, "What do you look like after lightning hits you?"

"I don't know," Nick said, "but I bet you don't look good."

They fell asleep during the flight to New York, neither waking until the descent into Kennedy. As the plane pulled up to the jetway, Bobby took out his pen and turned his ticket folder inside-out. "Autograph time," he said.

Five minutes later, as the line of disembarking passengers shuffled forward and turned toward the exit, Bobby peered into first class. Leary was still on board, awake and looking out a window.

"Hey, champ," Bobby said, "can I have your autograph?"

David Leary turned slowly from the window and stared, unblinking, at nothing. He seemed to listen for a long moment, like a man awakened by a sound he hadn't comprehended. When it didn't repeat, Leary turned away again.

"Let's go," Bobby said, his voice low, and he hurried his brother off the plane, unnerved by what he'd seen in the champion's face.

Leary thought someone had said something, maybe to him; he wasn't sure. He couldn't seem to focus on anything now.

He knew he was on the plane, sitting among other passengers, with New York and the night outside. But he was also back on the course near Philadelphia, watching the lightning reach down and into Jock, who stood erect for a moment, then toppled backward. Leary watched himself sprint the 150 yards and try CPR, but there was no life to revive. He saw himself kneeling in the rain next to Jock's body. Then the memory started over, and the lightning bolt reached down again ...

How long had this been repeating, he wondered. Seven hours? Eight? It began this afternoon, he was sure of that. On a golf course, time is measured by location, and he was teeing off on No. 10 when he felt the first raindrops.

More than 30,000 people had been on the course and

another 100 million had watched on television. What they saw was David Leary fulfilling every golfer's dream: six birdies and a 29 on the back nine, in the rain, to win the U.S. Open. He wasn't just famous now; he was a legend.

On every one of those last nine holes, he'd wanted to walk off the course. Once, on the 16th, standing over his tee shot, he'd picked up his ball and tee and was a half-second from telling the official scorer: "I'm done." Instead, with a sense of foreboding, he put them back down, and hit another perfect shot.

Leary had never believed in a god; he'd never believed in any other world than the one he could see and hear and touch. But now he knew there was something else out there, something capable of appraisal, judgment, and punishment.

The shots had all seemed easy, almost inevitable, and when the last putt rolled in on No. 18, Leary barely heard the cheers.

He knew what the sportswriters in the press tent would write. More than a few stories would begin something like: "David Leary, seemingly guided by a mystic hand, Sunday won the U.S. Open just four weeks after his caddie and best friend was killed by lightning."

For the past four weeks, the quiet words of sympathy had been constant. Everyone seemed to know about it. He and Jock had arrived in midafternoon at the Pennsylvania course to begin preparations for the next tournament. They walked the 18 holes, checked distances, worked out the likely pin placements, and discussed their strategy for each hole.

Then, using 200 of his own practice balls, the type he played in tournaments, Leary worked on his sand shots and chipping before sending Jock 150 yards down an unused practice area. Leary began hitting 8-irons, the club he hadn't been able to control the previous week. And he couldn't now, either.

Instead of each ball rolling to Jock's feet, the caddie had to keep moving left, right, forward, and back. And the old anger, the almost blinding obsession, began to rise again in Leary. "Failure is not an option," he told himself. He would stay there until he got it right, whether it took two hours or five.

Leary felt Flight 217 being pushed back from the gate at Kennedy International. Odd, he thought, that no passengers had gotten on or off, that there had been no announcements of landing or departure.

To block the memory of the lightning, Leary tried to think of Jock alive. He pictured the stocky Scotsman, redheaded, hard-eyed, and with skin weathered beyond his 59 years. Angus Muir's nickname had come from his teens and early 20s, when he'd made his living as a jockey. After he couldn't make the weight anymore, he'd moved on to another sport.

"The work's the same," he used to say, "only the title's different. Jockey for a horse or caddie for a golfer and you're still guiding a skittish beast around a course with a whisper in the ear and a touch of the whip."

Three years ago, in the first round of the Scottish Open at

Royal Dornoch, Jock was caddying for a young Austrian who was paired with Leary. On the 15th hole, Jock saw his golfer, in a bunker, surreptitiously nudge the ball with his foot into a better lie. After the round was over, Jock walked up to the young pro, who towered over him, and threw the clubs at his feet.

Jock put a finger on the man's chest and, in a loud, clear voice, said, "You're a cheat! I've never worked for one in my life, and I never will."

Jock waited a moment, giving the golfer a chance to argue or take a swing at him, but the only response was a weak: "Ah, you don't know what you're talking about, old man." The pro picked up his clubs and walked away.

Leary finished the tournament tied for 30th. After the final round, he was drinking at a pub near the course when Jock came in and walked up to him.

"Do you remember me?"

"I certainly do. Can I buy you a beer?"

"Maybe," Jock said, "but I want to tell you a few things first. Then you can decide about the pint."

"OK," said Leary, amused.

"First," said Jock, "I've never seen anyone punish himself so hard for bad shots. You hit one and you think about it the rest of the round. You never forgive yourself. Second, I don't think I've ever seen anyone play golf so stupidly. Golf is chess; it's just played on a bigger board.

"Third, I watched you play every round this week, and

you can feel when a 30-foot putt is one inch short. There are violinists who don't have hands like that. You should be one of the best players in the world, and you're finishing 30th in the Scottish Open." Jock stopped. Then he challenged Leary, "Now, do you still want to buy me that pint?"

Leary studied the little man's face for a moment. "What are you drinking tonight?"

They sat at the bar for the next three hours, talking, and the night ended with a handshake. Jock Muir had caddied on pro tours around the world and seen golf played at the highest levels. He agreed to work for Leary, but only for 26 weeks a year, and never more than three weeks in a row. "Because," said the Scotsman, "it wouldn't be fair to the missus."

When Leary met Helen Muir, she wasn't what he expected. She was an attractive, graceful woman, taller than Jock by a few inches, and although she was nearly 60, her eyes had the liveliness of a young woman's. Leary saw how she gently teased her husband and that, after 35 years of marriage, a subtle flirtation still went on between them.

They lived on Scotland's east coast in the village of Tayport, where Helen was satisfied to stay as Jock wandered the world. They never had children, and her days were spent as manager of a small tea shop.

"She says I've got an 'itchy foot,'" Jock once told Leary. "I developed a taste for the traveling back when I was riding. Helen understands, but she won't give me up for more than half a year. And I miss her too much to stay away longer."

Leary also learned about Jock out on the course and understood what it must have felt like to be one of the man's horses.

"In every race, there's a moment," Jock explained, "sometimes it's at the start, other times it's on the far turn, down the backstretch, or maybe at the wire, but you have to recognize that moment and you have to be ready for it, because that's when the race is decided."

A dozen times a round, Leary would be ready to gamble on a big shot, and the Scotsman would answer: "Not now." Then, perhaps on a par-5, from 270 yards out, Jock would hand Leary a fairway wood and say, "Now. Put it on the green, and the tournament's yours."

Every shot was discussed and planned with the next shot in mind. And on the greens, Leary was told to shut off his brain and feel the putter's stroke. "Your hands know what to do, lad. Don't get in their way."

Slowly the lessons were absorbed. Two saved shots a round moved Leary eight shots closer to the top of every tournament, and sometimes that was enough to win.

Leary respected Jock, and in return he received understanding. This, he sensed, was how fathers and sons were meant to feel. And, sometimes when Leary missed a shot, as they watched the ball soar off-line, Jock would grumble, "Ah, you bastard, you did it on purpose, just to make me

carry this damn bag a little farther. You're cruel to old men."
And Leary's fury would ease.

Throughout the flight to London, Leary kept Jock alive.

At Heathrow, Leary learned that all flights to Edinburgh had been delayed due to thunderstorms and fog. He rented a car, followed the roundabouts' signs to the M1, and headed north. It was Monday evening when he arrived in Tayport, and the day's rain had ended. The village, huddled close to the harbor, glistened as he made his way to the white, stone cottage.

Helen swung the door open. "David!" she exclaimed, surprised. Then she saw his haggard face. "What's wrong? Why are you here?"

"I need to talk to you."

She stepped forward and took his arm. "Come in."

Helen closed the door behind them and offered Leary a chair, then realized he was too agitated to sit. She let go of his arm and faced him.

"What?"

Leary had traveled 5,000 miles, and now didn't know what to say.

"David, what is it?"

"I don't know how to explain this. I don't know how people's minds work, but things get hidden, and then they come back, and you don't know what to do about them."

Helen took a step back, crossing her arms over her chest, fingers touching her shoulders. "What did you remember?" she asked unsteadily.

"Did you watch the tournament yesterday?"

"I stayed up till midnight watching you win."

"Since Jock died, I'd never been outside when it rained. Yesterday, on the 10th hole, it began raining ... that's when it came back."

Leary began talking faster, hurrying to get the truth out. "The day he was hit, I was hitting practice shots, and I wasn't hitting them right. But I was going to stay there until they were perfect — nothing was going to stop me. In the distance, behind Jock, I saw a lightning bolt, then another one, and Jock didn't see them because he was facing me. The wind was carrying the sound of the thunder away from us ..."

"Oh, no ..." Helen put her hand over her mouth.

"Jock was standing out in the fairway and I knew it was dangerous but I didn't care. I needed to hit those shots just right. It was the third lightning bolt that hit him. When I was kneeling next to him, I knew what I had done. And then, somehow, the truth disappeared."

"And yesterday ... " Helen said.

"... the rain brought it back."

Leary's words were now images for her. "He was in danger and he didn't know it," Helen said, stunned. "And you didn't tell him."

Leary didn't reply.

"You were hitting golf balls and you didn't want to stop," her words were gaining an angry edge. "I've stood at Jock's grave and cursed the fates for what they'd done, but I should have been cursing you."

She walked to the door, yanked it open, and turned back to Leary.

"The cemetery's only a few hundred yards away. Why don't you walk up there and tell Jock what you did to him? You, his best friend, the son he never had — you bastard!

"Do you know how Jock asked me to marry him? He said, 'Come, grow old along with me.' And I said yes. Now, because of you and your self-centeredness and your self-absorption, I'll grow old alone, and I'll die alone, too. Because of you."

She walked out the door and headed up the hill. Leary knew not to follow her now.

He sat, exhausted, in a wood-back chair and looked at the large room. A fireplace was at one end, with two comfortable chairs in front of it. In the middle of the room was a small dining table, and on it were a dozen letters, along with a box containing dozens more. Leary closed his eyes. He'd seen Jock writing those letters and mailing one each day back to Tayport.

Leary now felt the weight of what he had done. He had committed an unforgivable act and he would be chained to it for the rest of his life, and that, he thought, was what he deserved. Justified misery. He'd killed one person and ruined another's life. No words could apologize for that, but something had to be said before he left.

Leary stood and walked out of the cottage and up the hill. At the entrance to the cemetery, he stopped, aware again how it overlooked the sea. The view, like the graveyard, was useless to the dead, he thought, but a help for the living. He saw Helen kneeling in the cemetery. She stood, put two fingers to her lips, and touched the new headstone.

She walked to the cemetery's entrance and stopped a few feet from Leary. "Did you come here today to apologize?"

"No. I only came here to tell you the truth."

Helen turned and looked out to the sea. "Jock used to talk about you a lot, and many of his letters were about you. He worried about you, and he cared about you. He said that there was a terrible phrase, and you used it all the time ... " She hesitated.

"'Failure is not an option,'" Leary said.

"Yes, that's it," said Helen. "Jock said it hurt to see you punish yourself with that damn phrase, but he said it was finally fading. You were letting yourself be human, and he treasured that success more than any other.

"But there is something Jock never would have told you and I wouldn't have either, but now you need to hear it.

"Jock and I married in our 20s. I understood that he would be gone for a part of every year, but I didn't really know how it would feel to be alone so much. You tell yourself a lot of things when you're lonely, things you know aren't true.

"I was 26 and I told myself that I was too young to be alone, that I was a pretty woman who deserved better, who deserved a man's attention ... " Her voice faltered.

"It only lasted a few weeks," she said, "and no one knew about it, but when Jock came home, he could feel it. I told him the truth, and he asked me if I wanted to leave him. I said no, and that night I fell even deeper in love with him — because he forgave me." Her gaze did not move from the sea, but tears were rolling down her cheeks.

"If I tell you that I blame you and I hate you, that could be my revenge, because you would never stop punishing yourself.

"But I don't have that option. I surrendered it when I was 26 — when I accepted Jock's forgiveness. And I'm not going to give you a choice, either," she said. "I forgive you. And now you have no option — you must forgive yourself."

She turned, walked down the hill, and was gone. Leary looked out at the sea, bowed his head, and in a whisper that he thought only he could hear, said, "Thank you." ♦

Three
Stories

D avid Awtrey, walking down the aisle of Flight
889, stopped next to Row 22 and looked at
the unhappy 10-year-old who resembled him
so much.

"John, I've got good news."

The boy in Seat A, immediately suspicious, looked up at
his father.

"I just talked to the pilot," David said. "Because it's
Halloween night, he'll let you parachute out of the plane —
but only if you'll wear your costume."

John rolled his eyes in an I-knew-this-was-coming look.

"He says it would be a real thrill for the other passengers
to watch Batman parachute into Los Angeles. Actually, I'm
kind of looking forward to it myself."

"Dad, this isn't funny. We should have been home hours
ago. Now, because of that stupid car, I'm going to miss

trick-or-treating. And what's a transverse axle anyway?"

Their three days of rafting were now forgotten, David realized. His red-haired, freckle-faced son, whose black-frame glasses made him look like a very serious, miniature adult, was distraught about all the candy he wasn't collecting.

"Well," David glanced around the mostly dark cabin, "you could go trick-or-treating here on the plane. Of course, you'd probably just end up with a lot of peanuts and breath mints."

John leaned his head against the oval window and sighed.

"But I have another idea," David said. He paused, waiting until John, too curious not to react, looked up. "What if I told you a Halloween story instead?"

With the instincts of a businessman, John recognized a chance to negotiate. "How about three?" he countered.

"Only three? Why not 10 or 12?"

"Three would be fine," John said cheerfully. "But," his tone was now firm, "every story has to have an illustration."

"Are you sure you're only 10 years old?"

"Three stories, with pictures," John said. "Deal?"

David gave an exaggerated sigh and slid down into Seat B. "Deal."

John, triumphant, watched his father reach down and, from a small knapsack, pull out a sketchbook with "Awful

Productions" on the cover. David flipped past several dozen pages of cartoon characters, stopped at the first blank page, and took a pencil from his pocket.

"Now," David lowered his voice so that only John could hear him, "in all the rows behind us, did you notice that there are only three people with a light turned on above them? Well, I know something about those people. I know why each of them is on this flight."

John unfastened his seat belt, turned around, and, kneeling, peered over the back of his seat. In the darkness, the three faces stood out, each one eerily lit by an overhead light that turned eyes into shadows.

"There's a sailor four rows behind us," John whispered to his father, "then a guy with a beard behind him, and near the back there's an old lady with gray hair and glasses."

"Whose story do you want to hear first?" David asked.

John studied the faces. "The sailor," he said, sliding back down in his seat. "Why's he on this flight?"

David's pencil began to move.

"That sailor is gunner's mate 3rd-class Joe Givens of the USS Montana," David said. "And today is Joe Givens' birthday."

"How old is he?" John interrupted.

"Twenty. And this is also the anniversary of his enlistment, because Joe joined the Navy the day he turned 18." The pencil, moving deftly, showed a young man wearing a white T-shirt and dark pants, sitting, looking up at the sky.

"Joe Givens grew up in San Diego, the only son of a fisherman. On weekends and every school vacation, he'd get up at four in the morning to go out and work on the boat with his father. By the time he was nine, Joe could gut and clean five fish in a minute. And by the time he was 10, he knew he didn't want to be a fisherman, but he loved being out on the sea."

On the page, Joe's face was young and eager, his hair short and dark, and the chair he was sitting in had become part of a gun turret, its long barrel jutting out above him.

"Every morning," David continued, "when Joe and his father went out to sea, they passed the Navy boats in the harbor, and Joe knew the silhouette of every light cruiser, transport, destroyer, and battleship.

"By the time he turned 18, he understood that the Navy worked in three dimensions: on the water, under the water, and above the water. But he liked the smell of the sea too much to go down in a submarine, and flying didn't interest him. He wanted to be on a ship." The pencil added clouds to the sky. "Joe Givens was born to be in the Navy.

"His family was happy when he joined, and so were all of his friends. Everyone expected it. The only person who wasn't happy was his girlfriend, Beth, because she was afraid she'd never see him again. So Joe is going back home tonight to surprise her."

"I want to hear more about the ship," John said.

"The USS Montana," David smiled, "is a battleship, or

ROW 22, SEATS A & B

a 'battlewagon' as it's known in the Navy. Joe's one of 12 men assigned to a starboard-mount gun that fires five-inch shells. The men call it their 'quaker gun,' because every time it goes off, the recoil makes the deck shake so hard that it feels like an earthquake just hit."

If you draw for a living, you only need a glance to memorize a face. David completed the small details of Joe Givens' eyes and mouth.

"But, of course, Joe's biggest reason for enlisting was the war."

"War?" John asked. "What war?"

"Oh, sorry," David apologized. "I guess I forgot to tell you. Joe enlisted on October 31, 1942."

"What? That's not right! He'd be an old man!"

"Joe Givens never made it home," David said. "The Montana was in the Pacific Fleet, north of the Solomon Islands, when the Japanese planes attacked. In the first 10 minutes, all three gunners in Joe's crew were killed, so Joe jumped into the chair and began firing. He shot down five planes. He never saw the sixth one — it came in over the port side."

John turned around and, kneeling again, stared back at the sailor. "But he's here!" he whispered.

"Every October 31st, Joe Givens tries to go home again to surprise his girlfriend."

John slid down in his seat. "He's a ghost," he said, eyes wide.

"Yes, he is," said David. "Happy Halloween."

John was silent for nearly a minute. "Those other two people, the old lady and the guy with the beard, are they ghosts, too?'

"Oh, no, they're as real as you and me. But you don't have to hear their stories." David closed the sketchbook. "I want you to be able to get to sleep tonight."

"The guy with the beard," John said, "I want to hear about him next."

"Ah, the Norwegian." David opened the sketchbook to a blank page. "Now there is a man who does something frightening. Lars Thorwald is the world's best mountain climber. There are 17 mountain peaks in the world that are above 26,000 feet, and he's reached the top of all of them. Now, John, did you notice that Thorwald's wearing a heavy sweater?"

The boy nodded.

"Well, it's because the cold never leaves your bones after you've spent a night on The Devil's Own Mountain, and Thorwald spent 20 nights there. It was exactly a year ago today, on October 31st, when Thorwald almost died while climbing that mountain, and yesterday he found out why he almost died. That's why he's flying to Los Angeles."

David's pencil began sketching large fingers and knuck-les in the drawing's foreground.

"The Devil's Own is in Alaska, not far from Mount

McKinley. It's not nearly as high, barely 18,000 feet, but even so, no one can stay at that altitude for long, there's not enough oxygen. Only a few people have the extra-efficient body chemistries that can function at those altitudes. Lars Thorwald is one of those people.

"Three sides of The Devil's Own aren't that hard to climb. It's the east wall, like the north face of Eiger, that's brutal. The ice isn't stable, so what you're climbing on might suddenly break off the mountain and take you with it. Also, there are ice storms, hailstorms, snowstorms, rock slides, and avalanches. And, the rock isn't all hard, so when you hammer a piton into it ..."

"What's a piton?" John asked.

"It's a bolt with a hole in one end for a rope. But if the rock isn't hard enough, when you put your weight on that rope, the piton pulls out — and it's a long way down. So many men died trying to climb the east wall of The Devil's Own that it was named the 'Widowmaker,' and for mountain climbers, it has become the last great challenge in the world.

"A filmmaker named Martin Ross announced that he was going to make a movie about the first person to climb the Widowmaker. Thorwald was the world's best climber, so he had the best chance, but Ross also wanted to hire the Norwegian for his film because Thorwald, with his blond hair and thick beard, would photograph well. He looks like he should be standing on a mountaintop.

"A dozen other climbers were hired to carry food, climbing gear, and film equipment to base camps on the mountain at 8,000 and 14,000 feet. But after that, there would be just Ross, Thorwald, and two guides — a father who knew the mountain well, and his son who had experience in filmmaking and sound recording.

"The film began in the village of Flåm, Norway, where Thorwald lived and trained in the mountains around the fjord. The first scene was Thorwald saying good-bye to his wife and children.

"Ross was sure that this would be the best film he'd ever made, and he decided that the movie's theme would be 'man challenging nature.' Before they'd even reached 10,000 feet on the Widowmaker, Ross was thinking about the Academy Award for best documentary."

In David's sketch, the fingers and knuckles were now gripping an icy ledge. Below them, looking up, was a man with icicles frozen in his beard.

"The climb lasted nearly three weeks, and the final eight days were just Thorwald working his way up, with Ross and the two guides following. They endured two ice storms, and three times they had to sleep in litters hanging from the mountainside, while the temperatures dropped to 20 and 30 degrees below zero. On one of those nights, a rock slide swept over their heads, tons of rock missing them by a few feet.

"But, they kept going up and were within 400 feet of the

summit when Ross announced that it was too dark to continue filming. Thorwald, 40 feet above the others, came back down the rope that he'd just bolted into the mountain, and, until they fell asleep, they talked about tomorrow's assault on the summit.

"The next morning, Thorwald almost died. As he climbed back up the rope, three of the pitons pulled out, then all the others came loose. He would have fallen three miles to the bottom of the Widowmaker, but, 80 feet below, one of their ropes was bolted to the rock face. Thorwald grabbed it. He dislocated both shoulders and burned the skin off both hands, but he held on.

"Thorwald was alive, but the climb was over. They made it back to base camp at 14,000 feet, where a helicopter picked up Thorwald and flew him to a hospital in Anchorage."

Under David's pencil, Thorwald's eyes grew more intense. There was no doubt now that he was staring up at someone on the ledge, and he was about to pull himself up to that person.

"But that can't be how the story ends," John objected.

"It was," David said. "Until yesterday. That's when Thorwald was in Seattle, changing planes at the airport, and he happened to run into the two guides, the father and son who'd climbed up the mountain with him and Ross. The son said that it had always struck him as odd that Ross told him to change the camera's film that last night on the mountain.

"'We still had film left on the reel,' the guide said. 'Ross insisted we put in a new one. It was lucky he did.'

"But Thorwald knew it wasn't luck, he realized that Ross had never planned to make a movie about man conquering nature; what he'd always intended was a film showing man dying as he tried to conquer nature. And there's no time to reload while a man is falling off a mountain."

"Ross loosened the pitons!" John exclaimed.

"While everyone else was sleeping," David nodded. "He made sure that he'd have enough film to capture the terrible fall of Lars Thorwald. And Ross had always known what the film's title would be: *The Widowmaker*.

"Ross lives in L.A., and he's going to be at the airport to meet Thorwald, but he doesn't know that he's been found out."

David's pencil finished the sketch, which showed Thorwald, with focused fury, about to come up and over the cliff's ledge.

"We've got to get off the plane before Thorwald," John said. "I want to see what happens when he meets Ross."

"Good idea," David said. "We'll do it."

"Now, what about the old lady?" John asked.

David turned the page. "Well, that woman's name is Nancy Stearns. At least that's what it is this year. Last year, it was Maryanne. The year before that it was Lorraine. And before that it was Kathryn, Janet, Irene ..."

"She's going through the alphabet," John said.

"Right." David drew the oval of a face. "She decided to do it that way because it's easier to keep track of her names."

John quickly counted on his fingers. "She's had 14 names?"

"Right. Her real name is Alicia Hardesty, but she had to drop that, of course."

"Why?"

David smiled as he added the round, wire-rim glasses.

"Alicia doesn't need glasses, but she wears them, and she stays out of the sun to keep her skin pale. Every morning, with just a little makeup, she takes the color out of her cheeks and puts a little darkness under her eyes. And Alicia Hardesty might be the only woman in the world who dyes her hair gray."

"Why does she do that?"

"Because people would remember a woman in her 30s or early 40s who was with a man in his 70s. But if that woman were in her 60s, no one would notice her."

David's pencil began work on the eyes behind the wire-rim glasses.

"Lonely old men are always happy for a woman's attention, and lonely old men always have insurance policies that they bought when they were young."

"She kills them!" John exclaimed.

"One a year," David nodded. "Fourteen names, 14 husbands, 14 states. Alicia will arrive in a city, go to the library, and read the obituaries. First, she finds an identity for herself, and then she searches for the names of women who left husbands but no children.

"Alicia will buy a dog and start walking it on the widower's street, and, eventually, he'll be outside when she passes. Perhaps he'll be watering the lawn, or his flowers, and she'll ask if her dog can have a drink. They'll talk for a while; then a few days later, she'll be walking her dog again, she'll say hello, there will be another chat, and that time or the next, he'll ask her in for a drink. And Alicia Hardesty always says yes.

"The courtship takes a few months, and the marriage only lasts a few more, because the happy widower dies one night during dinner. You see, Alicia worked in a laboratory once and learned about a chemical called coropene that will stop a person's heart in 20 seconds and disappear into the blood in 30. And the only giveaway is that coropene tastes just like fresh tomatoes."

David's pencil outlined thin lips that were curled into a too-sweet smile.

"Alicia has done her work in Florida, the Carolinas, Texas, and all over the Midwest, but she's never been to California, and she's ready for a new start. She'll rent a room somewhere, and tomorrow at 9 a.m., she'll be at the Los Angeles Public Library, ready to start again. And, somewhere in Los Angeles, there's a widower who's watering his flowers and wishing he weren't so lonely."

John shivered in his seat and did not turn to look back as David finished the sketch that showed a woman with gray hair, dark at its roots, and steady, unnerving eyes.

The pilot's voice came over the loudspeaker, announcing that passengers should prepare for landing.

"I still want to watch Thorwald," John said.

"It could be pretty interesting," David agreed.

Flight 889 landed smoothly, taxied to the gate, and the passengers were soon disembarking. John and David walked out of the jetway, then stood to the side as the passengers sitting behind them came off the plane. A throng of people was waiting at the gate.

When gunner's mate 3rd-class Joe Givens came out of the jetway, a little blond-haired girl shouted, "Daddy!" and ran to the sailor. He picked her up and walked the last 30 feet to the crowd, where a woman with a baby sleeping on her shoulder reached up and pulled his face down to hers.

"He's not a ghost," John said, disappointed.

"I guess you're right," David agreed.

Alicia Hardesty appeared, and a white-haired man stepped forward. "Susan," he said, kissed her, and took the bag from her hand.

John looked at his father, who smiled and shrugged.

Lars Thorwald strode into view, saw the crowd, and slowed as he searched the faces. A hand in the back went up and the people parted for a cherubic man in his 40s who was about 5-foot-6 and weighed no less than 250 pounds.

"Hey, Graham!"

"Patrick!" The bearded man shook his friend's hand. "How's the world's best chef?" he asked in a hearty Australian accent.

John, staring at the rotund man, whispered to his father, "I don't think he's ever climbed a mountain."

"No," David agreed. "I'm sure you're right." He glanced at his watch.

"It's 9:30. We'll be home by 10 and, if your sister's really nice, maybe she'll give you five or 10 pounds of the candy she collected tonight."

"She won't," John said glumly as they walked down the concourse.

"Well, I have a suggestion," David said. "Offer to tell her three stories about the people on our flight, and I bet she'll pay you in candy just to hear them."

John considered this. "That'll work," he nodded, grinning. "And the price will go up with every story."

As they walked through the terminal, father and son passed the sailor and his family, and the bearded man and the chef. In the distance, they saw the old woman and her husband walking hand in hand, talking, though their words were lost in the hum of a hundred conversations.

"Arthur," the woman said in a soft, sweet voice, "if it's not too late, let's go to that Italian restaurant that just opened down the street." She slid her hand into her pocket and around the familiar brown bottle. "I'm told they make a wonderful pasta sauce — you can really taste the tomatoes." ♦

ROW 22, SEATS A & B

My Father's Gift

"The English couple in Row 30 wants some tea."

"Okay, I'll take care of them."

Janet Pierce and Donna Stapleton moved smoothly around each other in the forward galley of the 747. Lunch had been served and cleared away, and most of the passengers on the Christmas Eve afternoon flight from Brussels to New York were dozing, reading, or watching a movie.

The flight attendants, friends since meeting during their airline training two years ago, now shared an apartment on New York's West Side, but sometimes didn't see each other for weeks. Because seniority determines flight assignments and vacations, both women knew they would be working the holidays, so they had bid for the same December schedule.

Janet delivered the English couple's tea. On her way back up the aisle, she noticed an old man sitting alone in Row 22, looking out the window, lost in thought.

187

Janet continued up the aisle, then glanced back again before stepping into the galley.

"Donna," Janet said, her voice low, "did you notice the man in 22A?"

Donna leaned out of the galley and counted rows. "White hair, white moustache, expensive suit? What about him?"

"Well, he can't be flying because of work — he's too old," Janet said. "And he doesn't act like someone on vacation, either. There's something more, something else. You can see it in his face."

"Then why don't you walk back there and tell him you're curious and you've just got to know why he's on this flight?"

Janet pulled out a small tray, put some sugar packets and creams on it, and picked up the coffeepot. "Maybe he'd like some more coffee."

"Same thing," Donna said. "See you in an hour."

Janet filled three other cups on her way back to Row 22. The cup in front of the old man was empty.

"Would you care for more coffee, sir?"

He was still gazing out the window and hesitated before releasing his thought. He turned to her. "Pardon?"

"Would you like another cup of coffee?"

"Yes," he said, "that would be nice. Thank you."

His words, slightly accented, were in the rhythm of another language. Janet held out the small tray and he put his cup on it. "Were you visiting in Brussels?" she asked.

"No," he said, "I own a small piece of land on the coast of Belgium. There is one spot, beneath an old tree, that looks out over the water. Every year, at this time, I go there."

"Will you be celebrating Christmas with family?"

"Yes. Tonight there will be five generations at one table."

His accent was almost Russian, she thought, but gentler, and she noticed that in each letter "t," there was the hint of a "d."

She filled his cup. "And the children can't wait for tomorrow, I'm sure."

"They are excited," he said, "but they'll open their presents tonight, on Christmas Eve, after the big dinner." He took his coffee off the tray. "That is the Polish tradition."

"Is that where you're from? Poland?"

"Yes, from Nizkowice, in eastern Poland. Well, now it is. When I was born, the town was part of Russia. It belonged to Poland again when I left."

"When was that?"

"In 1920."

Janet had already placed his age at about 80. "You must have been just a baby."

"No," he said, "I was 14."

Janet did the mental arithmetic, then failed to hide her surprise.

"Yes," he nodded. "I'm 94."

"And you're ..." she looked at the empty seats next to him.

"Traveling alone? I am. My body's slower, but not my mind, not yet."

"Did you leave Poland to come to the United States?"

"Back then, we called it 'America,' but yes, we did."

"We?"

"My father and I."

"How long did it take?"

"Three and a half months."

"I didn't know it took that long to cross the ocean."

"The ship only took two weeks. It took us three months to walk across Europe."

"You ..." Janet faltered, "you walked across Europe?"

"We didn't have enough money for the railroad; we had no choice. Then there was the ship across the English Channel, and another from Liverpool to New York City."

"To Ellis Island?" she asked.

"Yes. Past the Statue of Liberty."

A passenger three rows back held up an empty coffee cup.

"Excuse me," Janet said, tilting her head toward the waiting passenger, "but may I come back and talk to you?"

"Yes," he smiled, "I would like that."

Janet filled the other passenger's cup, then returned the tray and coffeepot to the galley. Donna looked at her. "He didn't have a story to tell?"

"Would you cover for me for a while?"

Donna grinned. "Sure."

Janet returned to Row 22 and sat down. The old man was looking at what seemed to be a watch, then he handed it to her. There were no numbers on its face, just four letters, and instead of hands, a slender, metal arm wobbled but stayed on true north. She suddenly realized its significance.

"Turn it over," he said.

Carefully scratched into the bottom were "Jan Glodek," "Józef Glodek," and "1920."

"I am Józef Glodek," he said as he took back the compass and studied it. "This is what we followed, and I've kept it with me for 80 years."

"How far did you walk?"

"More than 1,000 miles, but I don't know for sure. You can't walk a straight line like you can fly one. You take any road you can find and just try to keep going west. But there are at least 2,000 steps to a mile, and 1,000 miles means 2 million steps."

"Why did you leave Poland?" she asked.

"No one in Nizkowice understood why we were leaving. 'Poland is finally free,' they said. 'We have our country back.' And they were right. For the first time in more than 120 years, there was a Poland again. Russia, Germany, and Austria, together, had conquered Poland and partitioned it in 1795, each taking the piece closest to them, but The Great War — World War I — gave us back our country. Then the Russians invaded us again, and it took another two years to push them out.

"The Battle of Warsaw, in August 1920, was the turning point. When the Russians began their retreat, we knew we were going to be free, and my father came home."

"But then the two of you left," Janet said.

"I didn't want to. I was only a boy, and I heard what everyone was saying. But my father disagreed. 'It's not over,' he said. 'It will happen again.' He understood that we were living on the battleground of Europe. If a western European country wanted to invade Russia, it had to go across Poland, and whenever Russia wanted to attack Europe, it had to cross Poland. You can't have families and farms on a battlefield.

"Most of Poland is flat, open country, easy for troops to march through. We were not like Switzerland, safe behind her mountains. I remember my father saying: 'We are a great country with great people, but we are in the wrong place.'

"In The Great War, when the Polish men were conscripted, my father was forced to fight for the Russians. He said it was almost embarrassing, they were so disorganized and ill-equipped. They didn't even have enough guns and ammunition. And during battles, when they radioed their troop movements, they didn't even put them into code.

"It wasn't long before my father's battalion was surrounded and captured by the Germans, who shot all the Russians, then sent the Polish soldiers to fight on the Western Front.

"For three years, my father fought and dug trenches for the Germans at Verdun, the Somme, and Passchendaele, until the fall of 1918. Then, when word came that they would be retreating, he wondered if the Germans would decide to get rid of the Poles like they'd gotten rid of the

Russians. One night, he crawled 300 yards across the no-man's land between the two trenches and surrendered to an American company.

"After the Armistice, other men came home with things they'd stolen or taken from the dead. My father came home with something more valuable — a piece of paper with the name and address of an American soldier.

"To get into America, you needed money, or someone had to sponsor you and vouch that you would not need the government's support. My father and the soldier, Thomas Stafford, exchanged several letters discussing how they would open a series of bakeries in New York. Then Poland's fight against Russia began, and my father went off to war again.

"By the time he came back, in September 1920, my mother had died in the flu epidemic, and there was a letter waiting for him, from the American. Stafford had written because the door to America was going to close. Immigration quotas would be adopted in 1921. My father found a ships' schedule, picked an arrival date, and sent a last letter to Stafford. In five days, we sold what we had and walked out of Nizkowice.

"Physically, my father wasn't well. How could he be, after six years of war? He wasn't a big man, and his lungs had been burned by phosgene gas. One day, when the Germans fired gas shells toward enemy trenches, the wind turned around and blew it back at them. There were no gas masks for the Poles."

"When your father came home, he must have seemed like a stranger to you," Janet said.

"He was. I was eight years old when the Russians took him. When he returned for good, I was 14. Then, because of him, because of this stranger, I was leaving everything I knew. I didn't want to go, but I had no choice. He was my father. I did what I was told.

"During that first day of walking, I kept hoping he'd change his mind, turn around, and go home. I watched him, and he never looked back, not once. At the end of that first day, I was farther from Nizkowice than I'd ever been before.

"We carried almost nothing — we'd sold everything to have enough money for the boat tickets. Along with a few days' food, we only had two blankets, some maps that were often wrong, the compass, and a calendar. At the end of each day, we'd find a place to sleep, in the corner of a field or beneath a tree, and my father would pull out the calendar and cross off another day. Then he would flip to the last page and stare at December 24th — the day we'd arrive in America.

"During the first week of walking, it was awkward between us. My father said almost nothing. He wasn't unfriendly, but he was remote. He wasn't used to having a son, as I wasn't used to having a father. Eventually, he began to ask me questions to find out who I was. And I think I surprised him, because I'd read a lot."

Glodek looked at Janet. "You probably don't know much

about Poland, do you?" She shook her head. "Well, we aren't like Russia. We weren't a nation of illiterate serfs. Back when the Roman Catholic priests came north, they taught us to read while they were teaching us religion.

"I walked behind my father, and I remember the day that he said to come forward and walk next to him. Of course, I wanted to hear about my family, so he told me about my mother and how he'd met her, this pretty girl from the next town, and how amazed he was that she would marry him, a baker from Nizkowice. And he told me about my grandfather, also a baker, 'who couldn't make a loaf without a lecture,' and was always talking to my father about God, family, honor, and country. My father said that he knew every speech by heart, but he never minded hearing them, for my grandfather believed every word. And as my father grew up, the words in his head gradually made more sense.

"We walked northwest, to Warsaw, and I couldn't believe that such a place even existed. Such big buildings, and so many people! We followed the Vistula River out of Warsaw, but when it turned north, we continued west, across Poland. We passed battlefields, thousands of graves, and forests leveled by shelling. I remember one farmer complaining to us that every time he tried to work his field, he just kept plowing up bones.

"It was mid-October when we reached Germany, and colder now. We went south of Berlin, through Leipzig, Kassel, and Köln, and the walking was getting harder on my father. He was coughing a lot, but we didn't stop. He showed me on the maps where he'd fought and where he'd endured the winters. He told me about the years in the trenches, about the mud and barbed-wire, and always sleeping with his coat over his head because of the rats.

"The Western Front ran 475 miles, from the North Sea to the Alps. Thousands of miles of trenches were dug on both sides as the two armies pushed forward and were driven back, sometimes moving into the enemy's old trenches.

"The farther west we walked, the more trenches we found, still held in place by sandbags. My father explained that every frontline trench was seven feet deep so that a soldier could walk standing up without getting hit by snipers.

"He told me how, one time, he was talking with three other soldiers and, after he walked away, a shell fell where he'd been standing, blowing those men apart. And of Christmas presents arriving for soldiers who'd already died, so their gifts were opened and shared by the living.

"But in the midst of all this misery, there was hope. On December 24th, on both the Eastern and Western fronts, one side would start singing Christmas carols, and the other side often joined in. Eventually, a local truce would be called, and these mud-covered men would climb out of their trenches and walk into no-man's land to sing and drink with each other and exchange souvenirs. That gave the enemy a face, and he turned out to be just another tired soldier who wanted to go home. Sometimes it took the officers eight or nine days to get their troops to start shooting again.

"I began to understand where my father had been and what he'd done. This quiet baker from Nizkowice, not yet 37 years old, had fought in two wars for three different armies, and he'd killed and nearly been killed. And now, every day, he was walking from sunrise to sunset to make sure that I wouldn't repeat his life.

"He told me what he'd heard and read about America. 'If you own a piece of land, no one can take it away from you,' he said. 'And if you have an idea, a good idea, you can grow rich.'

"And he talked about the holidays, the family that I'd have, what Christmas Eve would be like, the presents and the dinner, and how there must always be an extra plate at the table for someone who needed a meal — as we needed a meal right then."

"How did you survive on the walk? What did you do for food?" Janet asked.

"Out in the country, there were always fish in the rivers. And in the towns, we would follow our noses to the bakeries, and they often gave us yesterday's bread. Or we would exchange a half-day's labor for a few fresh loaves. At first, my father introduced me as 'Józef,' then, later, simply as 'my son,' and I liked hearing him say it.

"My body got used to the walking — at 14, you can get used to anything. But my father wasn't breathing well. He had to walk slower and rest more often, but he never complained and he would not stop. His coughing was nearly constant. I carried the compass and the maps and the blankets, and he followed me.

"From Köln, we went into Belgium, and it was less than 80 miles to the coast, but now he could only go a few miles a day, even if I was helping him.

"It was the evening of December 8th when we first saw the water, and I remember my father's smile — it was like he could breathe again. We were still in the countryside, and he sat down, leaned back against a tree, looked out at the sea, and smiled.

"'We did it,' he said. 'We made it.'

"'From now on, the ships will do all the traveling,' I told him. 'No more walking.'

"'No,' he agreed, 'no more walking.'

"We slept there that night, but the next morning he couldn't stand up. The coughing and the sound of his breathing were terrible. I think I knew then. We sat under that tree as his breathing got worse, and his face was almost blue from the lack of oxygen. In the evening, he said he wanted a promise from me.

"'Anything,' I told him.

"'I want you to promise that you won't go back.' He was my father, so, of course, I gave him my promise. He died a few hours later." Józef Glodek stopped and looked out the airplane window. He cleared his throat once, then a second time, and Janet put a hand on his right arm. He gave a half-nod and said, "I buried him there, with my own hands. The next day, I kept my promise, and I took the ship to Liverpool.

"There were thousands of us aboard the steamship that departed for New York, and so many languages that I'd never heard before. No storms came up, but the crossing was hard for me. I kept thinking that my father should have been there, for this was his dream, and he'd deserved a new start, a second try at life.

"We were three days out when I realized I might not get into America. Thomas Stafford would be at Ellis Island on December 24th, but he would not be looking for a 14-year-old boy traveling alone. He would be looking for his friend, Jan Glodek, and Jan's son. Stafford would not know me. And if you did not have a sponsor, you could be put back on the boat to Europe. I wondered how far it was from Ellis Island to the land, because I knew how to swim. Then I realized what a different thought that was for me. I was still 14, but I wasn't a boy anymore; you can't be after you've walked across Europe and buried your father.

"The ship arrived one day early, on December 23rd, and I remember our coming into harbor. The passengers were all standing on deck, but there wasn't any cheering or yelling. It was quiet. I think we were afraid because we'd come so far and still might not get in.

"We got off the ship and were put onto ferries that took us out to Ellis Island. The food was good, better than anything I'd had in four months. The men were separated from the women, and everyone was given a health inspection to make sure we weren't bringing any diseases into the country.

"I looked at all the people who were there, thousands waiting to be met, and I was sure I would be sent back. On Christmas Eve, eighty years ago today, I was sitting on a bench in the Great Hall when one of the interpreters came up to me, along with another man. The interpreter knew I was Polish, for we'd spoken before.

"'Are you Józef Glodek?' he asked.

"'Yes,' I said.

"The interpreter nodded and stepped back. The other man came forward and put out his hand to me.

"'I'm Thomas Stafford,' he said.

"I was dumbfounded. I didn't know how this had happened. 'How did you find me?' I asked in Polish. My question was interpreted, and I still remember Stafford's face as he searched for the right words. Then he said one sentence to the interpreter, who turned to me, and said, 'In your father's last letter, in September, he said you'd be arriving alone.'" ♦

Picture Perfect

S teve Kryder settled into Row 22, Seat A, and smiled. Sometimes, he thought, it all just comes together.

This weekend, he would be flying for 31 hours. And that was fine — in fact, it was great. Today would be New York to San Francisco, then San Francisco to Tokyo. Sunday would be the return flights, and he'd be back at the international equity desk on Monday morning.

Someone would ask, "Hey, Stevie, how was your weekend? You got any stories for us?" And everyone would look up, grinning, because Steve Kryder wasn't bashful about his love life. It was a man's world on the I.E. desk; women and sensitive souls didn't last long.

"Nothing to tell," he would answer, and there would be a chorus of boos. "But Mindy's coming into town next weekend." And there would be cheers. "You'll get a full report."

Then they'd all go back to their analysts' data and the news and numbers from the Asian markets, Zurich, Frankfurt, and London. Later, they'd call the portfolio managers, syndicate desks, and special clients and begin the salesman's pitch: "It's undervalued ... It's about to take off ... This is a good one." Now was the time for some company, some industry, something.

Every minute, someone made a fortune on Wall Street, and someone else lost one. And the difference, Steve had decided, wasn't brains — a lot of dummies were millionaires and a lot of smart guys went bankrupt. The difference was timing and luck, that's all, and the fates didn't care who you were. Life wasn't fair, Steve thought, and that's why he was going to Tokyo.

Flight 127 to San Francisco was almost finished boarding when a slender, blond woman started down the aisle, ticket in hand, looking at the row numbers. Come on, Steve urged, come on back to Row 22.

She was cool and sleek, and in her late 20s, he guessed. Her makeup was perfect, the tight, gray sweater would be cashmere, and he knew there'd be just a touch of perfume. Keep coming, Steve thought. She stopped at Row 22, faced him, then turned around and slid into a seat across the aisle.

So close. Steve watched as she put on her seat belt, and he decided that sometime during the flight he'd get a conversation going with her. After all, he had the looks — dark hair and an athletic build that looked good in Wall Street's uniform of button-down shirt, striped tie, and dark suit pants.

And she would notice the aura of success that he'd so carefully cultivated since his first month on the I.E. desk, when he had been told, "Act like you're rich and that your job is just a hobby." Of course, he wasn't rich; he didn't even have that first million, "starter money" as they called it. But he would tomorrow.

The plane's loudspeakers clicked and hummed, then the voice of the pilot, with an easy Texas twang, welcomed the passengers aboard Flight 127. Ten minutes later, the plane was angling upward into the clear March morning.

As the airliner climbed to its cruising altitude, Steve realized how weary he was: The last few weeks had been tiring and he hadn't slept well, but now he closed his eyes and, with relief, felt the familiar slide into sleep.

He felt someone sit down next to him, but he only rose to half-consciousness; then he relaxed again and disappeared into an even deeper sleep. When he awoke, he was leaning against the oval window and had to squint because of the bright, sunlit clouds. He wasn't sure how long he'd been asleep, but the nap had done the trick, his tiredness was gone.

He turned his head and visibly flinched. Sitting next to him, reading, was a girl, perhaps barely in her teens. When she felt him staring at her, she looked up. "Hi," she smiled.

He had to swallow to talk. "Hi."

"I'm sorry if I surprised you," she said. "I moved back

here while you were sleeping. The woman next to me had a baby with her ..." she paused. "You understand."

Her smile was friendly and unself-conscious. There are only so many traits in the world, Steve told himself, so they had to be repeated, over and over, and no combination was new. Here again were smiling brown eyes, light-brown hair, and the same young face of fine, balanced features. What had the girl just said? Oh, right, the reason she moved back here. "Sure," he replied, "five hours of baby talk would be enough for anyone."

"Unless the mother's paying me $10.50 an hour for baby-sitting. Then I'll give her all the 'goo-gooing' she wants."

This had unnerved him. Looking at the girl was like looking at Patsy. And this was how Patsy might have dressed — black jeans and a dark shirt and vest.

"You know," he said, "you look just like my sister did when she was 13."

"Thirteen! That's how old I am!" the girl in Seat B exclaimed. "How old is she now?"

"Thirty-five."

"Is she pretty?"

"Very," he nodded.

"Good!" she said. "Maybe I'll look like her. Do you have a picture of her?"

"Well, I ..."

"No," she interrupted, "I've changed my mind. Even if you have it, I don't want to see it!"

"Why?"

"Because then I'd know what I'd look like when I grow up."

"Aren't you curious?"

"Of course!" she said emphatically. "Everyone would like to look into the future, but I don't think anybody really wants to know what's going to happen. You know, it's like when you're reading a story — you're always wondering how it will end, but you don't read the last page until you get there. I mean, would you want to know your future?"

This weekend would set up the rest of his life, so he knew the answer. "I've got a pretty good idea what it will be."

"Is it what you want?" she asked.

"Absolutely," he said, but offered no details. The girl in Seat B waited a moment, then understood that this topic of conversation had ended.

"What's your sister's name?"

"Patsy — short for Patricia."

"Patsy," the girl repeated. "It's a nice name. Is she a nice person?"

"Yes," he nodded. "She's enthusiastic, with a lot of energy and a lot of friends."

"I bet you were best friends when you were growing up."

This wasn't a conversation he wanted to have, but he answered, "Yes, we were."

"Did you tell each other everything?"

"Just about."

"Is it still that way?"

"I live in New York City, and she lives upstate. We don't see each other too much anymore." Why, he wondered, did this girl have to sit next to him today?

"But when she needs something, does she still call you?"

"She's married now, with two children. Her husband's a good guy; she talks to him."

"It's probably not the same as talking to her brother," the girl said, then saw the uncomfortable expression on her seat-mate's face. "I'm sorry," she said. "I'm always nosy about people. I shouldn't pry. I'll let you alone." She waited a half-second for him to say she was wrong, then she smiled and returned to her book. Steve tried not to look relieved.

Thirteen years old. That was Patsy's age when we moved, he thought. And, he considered, that's really when this all began, while they were living in the brownstone in New York City. He was 12, a year and a day younger than Patsy, and Ellie was 15, and they were all sitting at the dinner table on a Friday night when their father said, "Your mother and I have some news for you. We're moving to upstate New York."

Their father, an executive with the telephone company, had just turned 40 and decided that life was too short to be wasted on a job he hated. He loved books and he'd always wanted to teach, so that's what he was going to do. And their mother wanted to get the family out of the city, so she was ready to go, but Steve didn't want to go anywhere. He was right at home with New York's energy, noise, and attitude. Sitting at the dinner table that night, he promised himself he'd get back as soon as he could.

The house they moved to sat on a hill overlooking Lake Ondaga, near Cooperstown. There were six bedrooms and a wraparound porch. The place was beautiful, but it was worse than just quiet, it was silent.

Steve had to wait six years to leave for college. He went back to New York City, to Columbia University up on 116th Street, and he wasn't going to leave again. It was different for Patsy and Ellie. They loved being out in the country. Eventually, they both married and had kids and lived within an hour's drive of their parents.

The land near the lake was never developed, and their father liked that you could still see the forests that James Fenimore Cooper wrote about in *The Last of the Mohicans*. Every high school in upstate New York taught at least a couple of Cooper's books, and that's what their father loved doing. He was everyone's favorite teacher, but he had to retire at 56 because of heart problems.

There was a good-bye party for him, and one of his first students gave him a painting of a scene that could have been from a Cooper novel. The setting was the bank of a churning, white river, and, in the shadow of the tall pines, a hunter in buckskin and an Indian stood next to a canoe, looking downstream, studying what lay ahead of them.

After their father retired, everyone was worried about

his health. But fate prefers the unexpected; their mother's illness and death caught all of them by surprise. Their father stayed at the house, but it was hard for him to take care of the property, so he hired Henry Russell, who'd been a janitor at the high school. Henry was in his late 60s and a little forgetful at times, but it was handy having someone drop by the house every day.

A few years later, as they knew it would, the heart attack came. It was Henry who found him on the porch, sitting in a rocking chair, a blanket around his shoulders, facing the lake.

The will named all three children as executors, and everything was to be divided evenly. They easily agreed to sell the house and, because it would look better with all the furniture in it, didn't touch anything until the place was sold.

In February, after the contract was signed, Steve, Patsy, and Ellie met to divide up the furnishings. They drew straws, and Patsy got the first pick, Ellie the second, and Steve the short straw, so he was third.

Their mother had always had a good eye for antiques, so the furniture, rugs, and artwork had a total value of over $90,000. Patsy, instead of taking the Shaker table or inlaid sideboard, used the first pick on the river-scene painting. It was unsigned and worth no more than $1,000, with most of that due to the gold-leaf frame, but the sentimental choice was in keeping with her personality.

As the three of them went through the house making their

picks, memories came back — of their parents, of Christmases, of relatives and friends. In this house, they'd shared secrets, problems, and laughter. And, until they'd grown up and moved away, they'd been each other's best friends.

By Sunday afternoon, everything of value or interest had been chosen. They began rolling up the rugs, packing boxes, and wrapping everything that was fragile. The river-scene painting was hanging over the living-room fireplace, and Steve was the only one who could reach high enough to get it down. When he took it off the wall, the frame came loose. Neither Patsy nor Ellie was in the room, but he managed to grab both the frame and the painting.

The ornate frame never had looked right, he thought, it always seemed too small for the picture. Now he saw that the frame had covered several inches of canvas on each side. More river, sky, and trees were exposed now, and something else, a signature — "Francis Bierman."

For the first time, Steve was glad that Columbia believed in a balanced education. Everyone, including finance students, had to take a few courses outside their major, and art history was one of the easiest. The professor had loved Bierman's work, and the most memorable fact was that anything painted by Bierman was worth at least $1 million.

Steve nailed the frame back on. Patsy came back in as he was wrapping the picture. They worked together, using heavy cardboard and brown paper, to protect the canvas.

And "just to make it secure," Steve added two heavy strips of brown tape. Patsy wrote her name on the package then put it with the other things she'd chosen.

He knew it was pointless offering to buy the picture because Patsy wouldn't part with it. And if he told her it was a Bierman, she'd insist that they declare it part of the estate, which meant they'd have to sell it just to pay the taxes.

Steve loaded Patsy's car until there wasn't enough room for the painting. On Tuesday, Henry would come with his van to take the rest of the pictures and small boxes to Patsy and Ellie.

Patsy had second thoughts about leaving the painting behind, but the lake house had an alarm system that was wired to the local police station. Steve and Ellie convinced their sister not to worry, and Steve went back to the city Sunday night.

On Tuesday morning, he felt like a character out of a Cooper novel, hiding in the trees near the lake house, but instead of a tomahawk or rifle, he had a cellphone and binoculars. This wasn't the first time he'd spied on people. He had a telescope in his apartment window in Manhattan, but it was strange to be out here in the country, spying on the house he'd lived in.

His plan was simple and perfect, and he'd come up with it before he'd even finished nailing the picture frame back on.

Henry arrived at 9 a.m., backed his van up to the house, and unlocked the front door. He turned off the burglar alarm and began loading the boxes. Not until the end did he bring out the wrapped pictures. The fourth one had two strips of brown tape around it.

Steve watched Henry carry out one more picture, then he hit the power button on the cellphone and punched in the telephone number of the house. The phone rang five times before Henry decided that he should answer it.

"Hello?"

"Henry, it's Steve. I'm down in New York City. How are you?"

"Oh, I'm pretty good. I've got no complaints."

"I just took a chance, thinking I might catch you there. This morning, I realized that during the weekend I forgot to look in the shed near the lake. Some things might have been left there."

"I'll check before I go."

"If you don't mind, Henry, would you do it now, while I'm on the phone?"

"Sure, Steve. Hold on."

Through the living-room windows, Steve saw Henry put down the phone and walk toward the back door. Steve sprinted to the van, pulled out the picture with the two strips of brown tape, and was back in the woods minutes before Henry returned to the living room.

"Steve, I just looked in the shed," Henry reported. "One of your sisters must have cleaned it out. It's empty."

"Thanks, Henry. I'm sorry to have wasted your time."

They said good-bye and, a few minutes later, Henry brought out two more wrapped pictures. He went back to the house, reset the burglar alarm, locked the front door, and left. Steve waited another 15 minutes, just in case Henry had forgotten something, then hiked the half-mile back to his car. Steve took the picture to New York and put it in the back of his closet.

The phone call came three days later.

"Steve," Patsy said, "have you been up to the house since Sunday?"

"No. Why?"

"The river painting is missing."

"It can't be. Ellie must have it."

"No. She's unwrapped everything that she took." From Patsy's voice, he could tell that his sister was on the verge of tears.

She told him that she'd looked through everything "four or five times" and that she and Ellie had spent an afternoon searching their parents' house.

"Nothing else is missing?" Steve asked.

"I don't think so. I've got everything else that I picked, and Ellie said she isn't missing anything."

"Who's been in the house since Sunday?"

"Only Ellie and me. And Henry — on Tuesday when he picked up the boxes."

"Is he sure he took the picture?"

"He says he took everything that had my name on it and

brought it all to my house."

"Did he stop anywhere on the way?"

"He thinks he only stopped once, in town, to pick up the morning mail. But he's not sure."

"Did he lock the van when he stopped in town?"

"He doesn't remember." Steve could hear Patsy crying. "I love that painting," she said.

They talked for another 20 minutes, and Steve said he'd drive up that night. The next two days were spent going through everything at the lake house, at Patsy's house, and at Ellie's. They met with Henry, but he didn't have an answer. Afterward, Steve asked his sisters, "If Henry didn't lose it, do you think he took it?" The two women said that was impossible; they trusted him completely. But Henry was the logical person.

A report was filed with the police, and an officer came out to the house. He interviewed Patsy, Ellie, and Steve, then he talked to Henry for more than an hour. Afterward, it was clear he thought Henry had the painting. He asked Patsy how far she wanted to pursue it, legally. She didn't know what to do.

The movers came the next week, and papers were passed on the house the following Monday. When Steve and his sisters came out of the lawyer's office, Henry was waiting there. He looked a lot older, Steve noticed. Henry asked if he could speak to Patsy, alone.

Later, she said Henry told her that because he'd been

entrusted with the painting and it was his fault for losing it, he wanted to pay for it. He gave her a check for $500 and said it would take him a few months, but he'd pay her the rest. Henry knew that the police thought he'd taken it, and he guessed the three of them thought so, too. He apologized to Patsy that he could never repay the sentimental loss.

Henry felt responsible and that was close enough to guilt, Steve thought. In fact, it was more than he'd hoped for; it was time to move on to the next step.

One of the great things about working on Wall Street, Steve believed, was that you meet all kinds of people. And if you want to do business with them, you find out what they're interested in. He had customers who thought he was fascinated by pottery, cricket, and dog shows. And that's why he knew that 19th-century American paintings were a passion of Masanori Murakami, the owner of several blocks of downtown Tokyo, and a man who could afford expensive hobbies.

Steve called Murakami and explained that he'd inherited a Bierman, but his sisters would be upset if they knew he'd sold it, so he was reluctant to put it up for public auction or sell it in the United States. Discretion was important; Murakami was very understanding.

It cost $4,000 to have the painting cleaned, and the result was breathtaking. Hidden beneath a century of smoke and dirt was the artist's genius, and now his brushwork and eye for detail were fully revealed.

Steve sent a photo of the painting to Tokyo, along with the

dimensions of the canvas. Three days later, a fax arrived, stating that Murakami was interested in seeing the picture in person. He would meet Steve at Narita International, accompanied by two art experts from Tokyo. If they gave their approval, Murakami would buy the picture for the asking price of $3.6 million.

Patsy would never know what the painting was worth, Steve thought. She believed she'd lost a $1,000 picture — and Henry was paying her back, so she was coming out even. Patsy wouldn't miss the money, and she didn't need it. After all, life was cheap in upstate New York; it wasn't like the city. Steve lived an expensive life, and he needed the money more than she did.

And, if Patsy and her husband had a hard time paying for their children's college tuitions, Steve would step in and help — they could count on it. After all, he and Patsy had been best friends. But what it all came down to was this: They weren't children anymore.

And that's why the hunter in buckskin, the Indian, and the river were all down in cargo somewhere, carefully packed in cotton and plastic and wood.

Steve reminded himself that he had to get rid of Murakami's fax, which was still in his desk drawer at work. He should have thrown the page away or run it through the shredder; for $3.6 million, it was worth it to do everything right.

Steve glanced again at the girl, who was still reading.

Even in profile, the resemblance to his sister was remarkable. It was almost funny, he thought, this girl sitting next to him on this flight; clearly, the fates had a sense of humor.

Flight 127 landed smoothly in San Francisco, and the line of disembarking passengers formed almost immediately after the plane stopped at the gate. The blond woman who'd been sitting across the aisle looked at the man asleep in Seat A. He'd noticed her when she came on the plane — she knew it — and she'd expected some kind of a move by him. Instead, he'd just slept the trip away.

As the last passengers left the plane, a young, female flight attendant stepped into Row 22.

"Sir, we're here." Gently, she shook the sleeping man's shoulder, but as soon as she touched him, she knew something was wrong. She put two fingers beneath his jaw; his skin was cool and there was no pulse.

She looked to the front of the plane, where the pilot was standing in the cockpit door. "John," she shouted, "we need a doctor! Call the terminal!"

She unfastened the man's seat belt and pulled him into the aisle, putting him onto his back. With her ear to his mouth, she watched his chest; there was no hint of breathing. She tilted his head back, lifted his chin, and began blowing into his mouth. Another crew member pulled a portable defibrillator out of an overhead storage bin, set it up, and prepared the paddles.

They pulled the man's shirt open and put the paddles on his chest. The defibrillator's sensors detected no heart movement and advised CPR instead of attempting a shock. A paramedic from the airport ran down the aisle, followed by a short, white-haired man, a doctor who'd been about to board another flight.

The finality was obvious. The doctor repeated the flight attendant's actions, checking for pulse and breathing, then he opened the young man's eyes. They were dilated, lifeless, and dry. "He's dead," the doctor said, closing the eyelids. "I can't be sure, but his heart was probably the cause. And he didn't die just now; it's been a while." He looked at the flight attendant. "I assume he was traveling alone?"

"Apparently. No one ever sat next to him." The flight attendant noticed a dark suit jacket in the storage bin above Row 22. She pulled it out and, from an inside pocket, withdrew a ticket folder. "Steve Kryder," she read. "On his way to Tokyo." A cargo claim ticket was stapled to the envelope. "I'll make sure we take care of this."

She gazed at the man who lay on the floor. "Look at him," she said. "He was young, good-looking, and from his clothes you can see he was a success. He had his whole life in front of him."

She shook her head and sighed. "Sometimes you wonder if there's any justice in the world." ♦

Mozambique

"Hello, Jack."

I stopped in the aisle of Flight 614, travel bag in one hand, and scanned the faces to my left, then to my right. I knew who I was looking for because you never forget some voices.

She was sitting in a window seat, a half-smile on her face as she waited for me to find her. My ticket was for a row farther back, but I was the last passenger to board the Chicago-Washington plane, and the seat next to her was empty.

I put my bag in the overhead storage bin, sat down in 22B, and kissed her on the cheek. Her perfume was still the same, and I've never forgotten it because I think of her every time I smell that scent on another woman. I'm glad that my wife has never worn it, for I would have asked her to change. You don't want to confuse the present with the past.

On physical beauty alone, it would be easy for any man

to fall in love with Anna Redden. Slender, with brown hair and blue eyes that seemed to have a light of their own, she was wearing blue jeans and a work shirt that didn't emphasize her figure, but couldn't hide it either. And, more important, she was one of the world's best news photographers. Anna had the ability to see a picture before it happened, to know how light and shadow would fit together an instant before it did.

I put on my seat belt and leaned back. She turned her face toward me and I turned to her, and it was as if our heads were on the same pillow again.

She was never the kind of woman to gush with excited chatter; that was one of the many things I'd liked about her.

"It's been a long time," she said.

"Eight years — since Jerusalem."

"Sort of. I saw you a month after that, at a conference in Washington, but we'd already said good-bye once."

She looked weary, and it was more than just the passing of the years between 28 and 36. She knew what I was seeing. "I'm not looking too good these days," she said quietly.

"Not at all, you ..." but she touched a finger to my lips and shook her head.

"How's your family?" she asked. The non sequitur was firm and deliberate.

"Good," I said. A mutual friend somewhere had probably provided an update on my life. "Marie is four and Jonathan is two, and I don't think there's ever been a mother who loved her children more than my wife, Elizabeth."

"And their father?"

"He kind of likes them, too."

"I always knew you'd be good at it."

I looked into the eyes of the woman who I once knew better than anyone on this earth, and I thought how easily it all could have gone the other way. Then there would have been no Marie, no Jonathan, and no wife who loved me daily, even while admitting she did not understand me.

A voice came over the aircraft's loudspeakers. "Good afternoon, this is Captain ..." the plane jolted slightly as a tractor began pushing it away from the gate, "... and I'd like to welcome you aboard our nonstop flight to Dulles International ..." A safety film played as we taxied out for takeoff. At the head of the runway, the plane turned into position and accelerated.

"Do you remember the 'airport' in Ethiopia?" I asked as we lifted off.

"And that little man with the moustache?" she smiled. "I can still picture him sitting in his old convertible next to that field, taking our tickets. And his wife — she must have been twice his size — in the back seat. How many airplane passengers can claim to have taken off, then watched the airport terminal drive away?"

Her pleasure in the memory restored some of the woman I knew. "But," she said, "I'm still waiting for someone to start a country that begins with the letter 'X.'"

FREDERICK WATERMAN

If you cover the world's news, you will see most of the
world. Once, in Qatar, Anna and I started counting up the
countries we'd been to, but we got bored after reaching 70,
so instead we tried to work our way through the alphabet,
country by country, from Afghanistan to Zimbabwe. We
were suddenly appreciative of Oman and Yemen, but we
never came up with a match for the letter 'X.'

"If anyone starts a 'Xanadu,' you can retire," I said, "now
that you've won the Pulitzer."

The smile died right out of her eyes. You don't know
where the trapdoors are if too much time has passed.

The prizes were announced three months ago, in April,
and no one was surprised to see Anna's name on the list.
She'd arrived in Europe at the age of 24, a freelance photographer who made her ambition clear: She was there to
win a Pulitzer. She should have won it her first year overseas, when she took the picture that summed up the war in
the Sudan. The photo showed a group of African children,
none more than six years old, holding pistols and standing over
the body of a man they'd just shot. I am sure that it didn't win
because it was too good; it was too unsettling to see blood
lust in babies' faces.

I looked at Anna. Eight years had passed, and we still
weren't strangers. Do you ever really stop loving someone?
If there was enough kindness and passion, I don't think the
warmth ever goes away completely. I looked at her hands,
and there were no rings.

When she first arrived in Europe, I was already working in Paris as the overseas correspondent for a Chicago newspaper. Within a month, I asked her to share my apartment, and she easily joined the band of reporters, photographers, and video cameramen who traveled together. It was a hardworking, lighthearted bunch that included Americans, Brits, Italians, Dutch, Swiss, and a couple of crazy Aussies. Someone called us the "Gypsy Moths," and the name stuck because that's what we were, a bunch of journalist gypsies drawn to the day's brightest story, which we circled until it dimmed, then we were gone.

No matter where we went, to Cairo, Karachi, Istanbul, wherever, we'd inevitably end up at a bar together, entertaining each other with stories of where we'd been and what we'd seen. Once, far past midnight, a bartender asked how we found the next big story. "It's simple, mate," said one of the Aussies, "we just follow the Four Horsemen of the Apocalypse: famine, flood, pestilence, and war." An offhand reply that was dead on-target.

Every group has a personality, and the Gypsy Moths were like a sports team: you kept a layer of bravado on the surface. And whether your story that day was about a child beggar; a young woman taken away by soldiers; or a prisoner marched over a hill, and the sound of a single shot, at night you were laughing in a bar.

I liked the restless life — the excitement of waking up every morning and wondering where I was and why I was there. Adrenaline is addictive, don't let anyone tell you it isn't. For most people, one year is very much like another. For overseas journalists, no year, no month, is like any other. We lived from headline to headline, with a bag always packed and next to the door.

And when there was a lull in the news, it made us tight and irritable, like racehorses left in the gate too long. Then, there would be a rumor, a whisper, a bulletin, and we were off again. I cannot disentangle Anna from the excitement of that time, for I loved them both.

She and I never talked about the future; life is simple if you just focus on today. Her goal was a Pulitzer, and mine was to cover the White House. When I was reassigned, we pretended we were different from ordinary people, different from the "civilians" whom we photographed and wrote about. We'd spent four years together, but there would be other loves down the road. We wished each other luck. We made the good-bye too easy.

"Do you still have the apartment on the Boulevard Montparnasse?" I asked.

She shook her head. "I gave it up last month, before coming back to the states for my sister's wedding. Elaine finally married Will."

"So, where next? Asia? South America? Or stay here for a while?"

"None of them. I'm catching a connecting flight this evening, out of D.C., to Johannesburg." She stopped and,

for the second time, abruptly redirected the conversation.
"What about you, Jack? Am I right in guessing that the
White House correspondent just finished checking in with
the home office?"

I nodded. "Three times a year, I go back to Chicago and
spend a day with the editors. We talk about our national cov-
erage and what Illinois' congressmen and senators are up to,
then during lunch I repeat all the beltway gossip I can
remember — that's probably the real reason they want to see
me."

"And they haven't tried to make you managing editor?"

"There were some hints last year, but I had the job I'd
always wanted. Now ... I'm not so sure. The president likes
to travel, and I think I've had enough."

She was only half-hearing me, and I wondered how far
her thoughts were from my words. "What's wrong?" I
asked.

She gave me a pained, pleading look that I recognized. I'd
seen it once before, on the face of a man who'd caused a car
crash — three people died, but he'd survived without a
scratch. Anna sighed. She was too weary not to tell the truth.
"When you can't get to sleep at night, you have to resolve
the reason why, so I'm going back to Mozambique."

That, I knew, was where she'd found her Prize-winning
picture. I didn't prod her to continue; she needed to go at her
own speed.

"You remember the floods last year," she said finally.

"When they kept getting worse, I took a flight from Rome down to Tanzania, then I hired a plane to take me into Mozambique. It was still raining in the southern and central provinces, and every landing strip was under water, so we flew up north, to Niassa, where the rains had stopped. I took some aerial shots, then my pilot found a straight piece of road that was almost dry, and we landed. I wanted to walk around and look for something good.

"I found what used to be a village. No building was standing, and nobody was there. I guessed that everyone was still up in the hills, where it was safe. Only a few structures had been made out of wood — not many people could afford it. Everything else was made of mud bricks, and when the water swept through, it washed away those houses like a garden hose hitting ant hills. All the wood structures collapsed.

"I was walking past a pile of debris of what must have been a big, wood-frame house when a man's voice called out. I looked over and, right in the middle of a pile of boards and beams was a dark triangle of shadow, with two eyes looking at me. I didn't understand the man's words, but I knew he was begging for help.

"Then I saw what a great picture it was. There was shock and anguish in his face, and his tears had tracked down through the dirt on his cheeks. His skin and hair were so dark that they blended into the shadows. It was as if the building had a soul and it was staring out at me.

"So, what do you do? Do you grab a board or a beam and try to get him out? Or do you pull out your camera and check the light? You know, just a few shots — and you hope he won't close his eyes because he'll ruin your wonderful picture. And perhaps he realizes that, and wonders if it's the price for your help. If he turns his head or closes his eyes, and you don't get your picture, maybe you'll walk away — and the next thing that goes past might be animal instead of human.

"So, what do you do? Pick an f-stop or grab a board? What will it be? Who are you, really?"

"I remember the picture," I said quietly.

"My wonderful Pulitzer Prize," Anna said. "Over the next 10 minutes, I took a full roll of film, using different lenses and exposures, then I went to get the pilot to help, but I found a group of local men first, and they came back with me. In the time I was gone, the pile had shifted. The triangle of shadow was gone, and the man was deeper inside. I could hear him talking, and his voice was so soft ... he was praying.

"The men took the wood off carefully, making sure that nothing else fell on him. When they pulled him out, he kept looking at me, and I knew what he was thinking: I'd shown him who I really was and what was really important to me."

"Your job was to get the picture," I argued.

"Then I did my job — but that picture is what I see every night when I try to go to sleep," she said. "Sometimes, in my worst dreams, that man and I can suddenly speak the same language and he is back inside that building again, trapped, asking, 'Do you want me to cry some more? Would that help?' Other times, it's like a fashion shoot. I've set up lights on tripods, and I'm moving around, saying: 'Beautiful! Fantastic! You're perfect!'"

Anna exhaled slowly. "It was late afternoon when they pulled him out, and the pilot's home airfield didn't have lights, so we had to leave. One of the men wrote down the name of the village and the name of the man who'd been trapped. He was a friend of theirs, and they took him with them. Three days later, when I was back in Paris, I called the pilot and asked him to find out what happened to the man in the house. I was told that he died a few hours after we left."

Anna turned away from me. In four years, I don't remember her ever needing comforting. I put an arm around her, and she leaned into me.

"History needs witnesses," I said.

"I can't wrap myself in that," she replied, wiping her eyes. "It was never that noble, not for any of us. I remember all of us sitting in a bar, wishing for a war — somewhere, anywhere."

"Why are you going back to Mozambique?" I asked.

"Two doctors from France, a husband-and-wife team, are going to open a clinic in Niassa, not far from where that man's house stood. They'll do the medicine and I'll do the administration."

I understood that part of her was already there, waiting where the house had stood. I reached out and took Anna's hand. For the next hour, we ignored our thoughts and talked instead about the news and of old friends, and even when we weren't talking, she held my hand in both of hers. When our flight touched down at Dulles International, we let each other go. We walked off the plane and there was no talk about getting together, no suggestion of staying in touch. At the gate for her next flight, I kissed her on the cheek, and hugged her, and we said good-bye again.

I walked down the long concourse and, beyond the security barrier, saw Elizabeth, Marie, and Jonathan come to surprise me. Jonathan saw me first and started shouting. I walked past the checkpoint, then kneeled down and picked up my son, who began telling me, in a hundred words he couldn't quite say, about all the planes he'd just seen. Then my daughter wrapped her small, sweet arms around my neck.

I stood up, holding the two of them, leaned forward and kissed my wife gently on the lips. Then I kissed her a second time, and read the surprise in her eyes. Without saying the word, she asked me, "Why?"

"Because I saw a friend today. She's going to Mozambique, and I'd like to tell you why." ♦

Best Man Wins

I walked onboard Flight 587 from Paris to New York, showed my ticket to the flight attendant, then walked though first class, where I usually sat, and continued back to coach. At Row 22, I stopped and looked down at the man sitting in Seat A, the man who I knew would be there, the man who had been having an affair with my wife for the past four months.

I sat down in Seat B.

Jean-Louis Vachon did not look up from the pages of *Le Monde*, for he was not a man to be bothered with nods of hello to other travelers. I have known him for nine years, but I wasn't sure how I'd react this time. Five days ago, a computer at home malfunctioned, restoring a hundred deleted files. My wife's words to Vachon left no room for doubt.

What did I feel? Rage, bitterness, bewilderment, and sick despair each took their turns with me. I have not told her that

I know, but each day I struggle to hide my anger, while every night my best and sweetest memories of love are turned into nightmares — with the Frenchman in my place.

I'm trying to think clearly now, trying to get back to who I am. I want to know who to blame. Her? Him? Probably both. Revenge is tempting, but I'm going to solve this problem for good.

The wedding ring on my left hand still looks new. Our impulsive, romantic marriage took place three years ago, in a small, stone chapel outside of Paris. At the post-wedding dinner, I remember my best man, Jean-Louis Vachon, saying how envious he was, for I was marrying "the most beautiful woman in the world." I didn't know how deep his envy ran.

I glanced at Vachon. If I waited too long to greet him, my presence would seem ominous, and he would guess that our seat assignments were not by chance.

I took a deep breath. "Jean-Louis! Is that you behind the newspaper?"

He turned to me. "Edward, my friend! They have given you this seat? How lucky for me!" His charming smile was now in place, but I had seen a flicker — not of guilt, for Vachon would have none of that — but animal alertness.

"It's wonderful to see you, Jean-Louis. It's been too long." What, I'd asked myself last night, should a cuckold sound like when he's sitting next to his wife's lover? I would try for one-part happy, two-parts ignorant, with a thin coating of fool.

"How are the Vachon vines?" I asked cheerfully. "Provence is getting good weather this summer, and I've heard two vintners say they are dreaming of another year like 2000."

"We are all dreaming of another 2000, though it may not come in our lifetime." Vachon's English was perfect, but his words still rode a French cadence. "Men who grow grapes are always at nature's mercy."

I smiled at the man I hated. "Jean-Louis, at Les Mirettes my customers don't even look at the wine list anymore. They only want to know if I have 'Vachon.' I might as well take the rest of the wine cellar and throw it into the East River."

"Let me know the day, and I'll help you. I'm always glad to get rid of my competition. But, Edward, as a wonderful chef, you will never have that problem. You have no competition."

Vachon, I thought, you are playing a little game with your words — you are my competition, and you know it. But I let no recognition come into my face while the Frenchman enjoyed his private double-entendre.

The last, breathless passengers arrived on Flight 587. The usual announcements were made as we taxied across the tarmac, and the plane barely paused at the head of the runway before accelerating, lifting off, and angling upward.

Vachon traveled frequently to the United States and often came to my restaurant, though not in the past four months. Now I knew why.

"Jean-Louis, it's been too long since you've been to Les Mirettes," I said, with a cuckold's amiability. "I can't tell you how much Carolyn enjoys seeing you."

Vachon studied my innocent face and relaxed completely. He was safe. "You are a lucky man, Edward, being married to Carolyn. If you ever get tired of her, give me a call."

And there was the problem: I wasn't tired of her. Four years ago, blond, blue-eyed Carolyn, whose face had looked out from a hundred magazine covers, came to my restaurant with a group that I knew. They invited me to join them for a drink, and I sat next to her. As we talked, I remembered her pictures because her eyes had an intelligence that, through the makeup and poses, seemed to say, "Isn't this silly?"

She treated her beauty like an inheritance — unearned, but appreciated. Of all the models who came into Les Mirettes, Carolyn was the only one who I never saw glance at herself in the long mirrors. She was from South Dakota; I grew up in Brooklyn. We were country and city, but from that first evening, the chemistry was good. The following night, at my invitation, she returned to the restaurant alone. And the next night, she ended up eating in the kitchen, talking and laughing with my crew, who threatened to quit en masse if I let her get away.

I was 34 when we made that impetuous marriage trip to France, and Carolyn was 24 — young enough to make the age difference interesting.

There is one, invaluable skill that I think comes easier

when you are from a city: the ability to talk to anyone, and a successful restaurant owner must know how to work both the stove and the crowd. But how do you handle seven hours with your wife's lover? What do you say — "What's new? How's your business? How's my wi..."

Stop it! I told myself. But the anger, so alive it had a voice, whispered to me, "He's right next to you! One punch! Do it now!" At this range, I could knock Vachon out with a single blow. Afterward, I would quietly tell the flight attendants, "Shhhh, he's sleeping." And if he started to come around? I could hit him again. What husband would not be tempted?

It is impossible not to compare myself to Vachon, to ask: Who is truly the best man? I will concede right now that he is far better-looking. Vachon is handsome in a sleek, self-aware way and possesses an almost courtly demeanor. "Half-prince, half-tennis pro," is how someone once described him. Vachon looks like men wish they did; I look like they do. I look like the man who comes to fix the washing machine.

But there are similarities between us. We are both driven men who have become rich because people will pay well to satisfy the whims of their taste.

Fifteen years ago, Vachon inherited the vineyard from his father. He understood how good the wine was and how underpriced it had been, so he cancelled the vineyard's long-standing European contracts, came to the United States, and began selling only to restaurants — at 10 times his father's old price. And he made a killing.

"Vachon vines" now have cachet and are one of the standards by which the top restaurants distinguish themselves from the second tier. Vachon has made his name famous — and I know how much that pleases him.

High above the Atlantic, the brilliant August sun turned the white clouds below into an ethereal wonderland. I was not in the mood for beauty.

"Jean-Louis," I said, idly turning the wedding band on my finger, "I'm surprised to find you here, flying in coach." In fact, I'd been astonished when my travel agent located the Frenchman's reservation.

He responded with a "What can you do?" shrug. "I had a meeting this morning in Montrouge that could not be changed, and I must be in New York tonight. This is the only flight that fit into my schedule, and first class is sold out. And what is your excuse, Edward?"

"A last-minute reservation," I answered, and it was true — somewhat.

Yesterday, the owner of Les Tifs mentioned Vachon's arrival from Paris. I called my sous-chef, told him he was running the kitchen that night, and gave him a list of instructions. Four hours later, I left for Paris — for the sole purpose of taking this flight back, in this seat.

Why, I've asked myself a thousand times, did the affair happen? Carolyn and I had fought no fights, had suffered no silences. I had not cheated on her, nor, I thought, she on me.

For the first two years of our marriage, Carolyn only went

on one-day photo shoots. But, I was rarely home, my life was at the restaurant. During the past year, she went back to a full schedule, including location shoots in Bali, Tangiers, and Rio, and runway work at the fashion shows in Milan and Paris. There was too much distance, too many nights apart. Either you're together or you're not; that's one of the basics, and both of us had missed it.

A salesman doesn't sell a product, he sells himself, and Vachon never stops selling. How can a woman tell which whispered words of love are real, for winning a woman's heart is the greatest sales pitch of all.

"Jean-Louis, my friend," I said, "you are remarkable. Who else could make his wine the most popular one in the United States without ever hiring a salesman there?"

"I worked hard those first two years," he said, "taking the wine myself from restaurant to restaurant. That was before the dinners, of course."

Among restaurateurs, an invitation to a Vachon dinner is as prized as an invitation to the White House. Every April, Vachon gives eight dinners: four on the East Coast, two in California, one in Chicago, and one in Texas. His guests are the men and women who own the finest restaurants in the United States. We are each asked to invite someone else, and we always do, for every meal is an epicure's feast, and every course is designed to complement the Frenchman's wine.

At the dinners, Vachon, always wearing a dark, European-cut business suit, listens intently to every owner's words, flirts just the right amount with every woman, and never mentions the business of wine — not once. But, a week later, one of his staff will call from Provence and ask if the restaurant is interested in placing an order. Once, an owner said "no," and he never received another call from Provence, nor an invitation to dinner. No one is sure if the story is true, but no one will take the chance that it isn't.

It was at one of these dinners that Carolyn first met Vachon, and there was no connection, no chemistry between them. After Carolyn and I sat down, with a mischievous smile she began whispering interesting possibilities into my ear. New love is a fine and imaginative thing.

At the following year's dinner, after we'd been married, I saw Carolyn looking at Vachon, appraising him. Later, when the three of us were talking, I noticed that her arms were crossed in front of her — a barrier in body-language terms.

This spring, after dinner, while I spoke with three other restaurant owners, Carolyn talked with Vachon, and this time there were no crossed arms. Twice, my wife touched his shoulder as she laughed; I knew that gesture, and its touch. Afterward, in the taxi, Carolyn never mentioned Vachon, but she talked a little faster and her words came out a little brighter. That's what she does when she's trying to hide her thoughts. I've never brought this flaw to her attention.

In the past four months, I heard that extra animation in her voice a dozen times, but I always ascribed it to the wrong things: to a gift, to a birthday, to the moment. I never reached for the larger answer. I never thought the unthinkable.

In summer, the time difference between Paris and New York is six hours. Flight 587 left at 12:55 p.m. and would arrive just before 3 o'clock. The timing would be perfect.

I worked the conversation with Vachon until we were talking like brothers, discussing his business, my business, the latest strikes in Paris, and a dozen other things. I marveled at how cool he was, joking and laughing with the man whose wife he was bedding.

The inflight movie was a thriller and, to my relief, a long one. Afterward, I again talked with Vachon about every subject that would interest him — but one — until the plane touched down at Kennedy International at 2:59 p.m.

"Jean-Louis," I said as we walked off the flight, "it's 9 o'clock in Paris, we're both hungry, and New York has a thousand restaurants. Let's find a good one and have a great meal."

"Ahh, my friend, I like the way you think. You make time for life's pleasures. How fortunate that we share the same tastes." His words were filled with self-amusement.

A car and driver were waiting for Vachon and, during the ride into the city, we discussed our restaurant options. We each suggested a dozen names and considered Bartolo's, Sierra Leone, and Jacquie M. before Vachon finally offered the compliment I was waiting for: "Edward, your restaurant is better than any of those."

"Then it's decided," I said. "I will make the food, and we will drink Vachon wine."

"The perfect meal," he agreed.

I leaned forward and told the driver, "54th and Lexington, please."

When we walked into Les Mirettes, I was reminded again how much a restaurant, in its off-hours, feels like an empty, theatrical set, waiting for the actors to arrive. Here, it would have been performers in a French play, for the restaurant's high ceilings, tall paintings, and cream-colored walls with gilt touches have elicited more than one mention of Versailles.

The time was not yet 4 o'clock; even the earliest dinner customers wouldn't arrive for another two hours. One of my instructions was for the kitchen staff to complete today's prep work by 3:30, then take a break away from the restaurant — mandatory.

Vachon followed me from the luxury of 18th-century France into the stainless-steel, operating-room cleanliness of the kitchen, where pots hung overhead, the floor was easy-on-the-feet rubber, and the refrigerators and freezers hummed together.

I exchanged my clothes for chef's whites, then from the temperature-controlled wine cellar at the back of the kitchen took out a bottle of Vachon wine. While the original owner opened it, I set up two wine glasses on the metal counter between us.

From the walk-in refrigerator, I took a flat, plastic Lexan box that had two loops of clear tape around it. My name was written in block letters on a piece of paper that I crumpled and put into my pocket. I sliced the tape, appreciative of how well my sous-chef followed orders.

"Jean-Louis," I said, "have you ever tried amontillado?"

Vachon did not look up from the glass he was pouring. "That little sherry from Spain? I choked a glass down once because the silly woman who gave it to me was pretty. Why do you ask?"

"I remember reading about it once," I said, "but I've never tried it."

I took the glass of syrah that Vachon handed me, swirled the wine in the small bowl, then brought the glass up to my nose. The aromas of fruit and earth triggered my salivary glands; I was tasting the wine before it reached my mouth.

"Outstanding," I acknowledged, enjoying the wine's long finish. I took a second sip, savored its three distinct stages of taste, then put the glass aside. From the Lexan bin, I removed several smaller, plastic containers and a package wrapped in wax paper.

"Jean-Louis," I said, "you've always succeeded in enjoying life to the fullest."

"Life is for the living," he replied, holding the glass of wine up to the overhead light and studying its reddish-plum color. "I want to die with a smile on my face."

I'd be surprised if you did, I thought.

"But, Edward," Vachon continued, "you, too, are living well. After all, you are the best chef in America. What did that food critic write? That you cook like someone who 'knows 12 languages and can mix the words together into a new language that only he can speak, but everyone can understand'? With you, every meal is like a trip around the world."

Vachon, the master complimenter, I thought. And so I stole his tactic.

"Jean-Louis," I said, "sometimes I think that before people sit down to dinner, they should be required to sing at least a chorus of '*La Marseillaise.*'"

Vachon's eyebrows rose in question.

"After all, it is France that gave us all the great sauces, pastries, bouillons, and stocks. And, after doing that, France gave us the best wines to go with every dish. Without your country, there would be no great food." Someone once told me you'd probably get physically sick before the recipient of a compliment thought you were being too effusive.

"Ah, Edward, what can I say?" Vachon replied, as if my praise had been given directly to him, instead of three centuries of chefs and vintners. "The French just know how to live. We appreciate the best things in life."

While Vachon talked about his country's magnificence, I began cooking. I opened one container, poured the pork and noodle broth, with shrimp, into a saucepan and turned the stove's burner to a low heat.

The second container held leeks and mushrooms. I stripped the leaves off a sprig of thyme, mixed it with ground mustard seed and Szechuan peppercorns, then added these seasonings. I put the completed dish into a saucepan and set the heat at simmer.

From overhead, I took down a low, wide pan, put in olive oil, and turned on the flame. I prepared and added, in order, garlic, onions, bell peppers, eggplant, zucchini, tomatoes, herbs, saffron, and finally pignoli. Vachon nodded in approval. "Ratatouille," he said. "Provence's other great export."

I pulled out a knife, checked the sharpness of its point and edge, unwrapped the wax-paper package, and took out the wide, flat fish. I sliced off the head and tail and dropped them into the shiny trash bin below the cutting board. I gutted, skinned, filleted, and pan-seared the fish, brushed on a hot-ginger glaze, and put it into the oven for a few minutes to caramelize.

From shelves near the dining-room doors, I took two large plates, two soup bowls, two linen napkins, and a handful of silverware. I served the broth, then the food. The aromas were as good as I knew they'd be.

Vachon took his first taste of the soup, closed his eyes, and said, "Amazing!" After another few spoonfuls, he could not wait any longer for the food. With almost gluttonous speed, Vachon picked up a fork and tried the fish, then moved on to the leeks and mushrooms, and finally the ratatouille. He was torn between savoring each bite and hurrying to the next one. I enjoy watching people eat what I've prepared; this time more than ever.

In just a few minutes, Vachon was halfway through each dish. That would be enough.

"You know, Jean-Louis," I said, as if a thought had just come to mind, "a beautiful woman is a remarkable creation, and there is nothing like the effect she has on a man."

Vachon, between bites, grinned at me.

"After all," I continued, "that's why you're still a bachelor, because of all the beautiful women. Every man who marries wants to marry a beautiful woman — but he forgets that after he walks his wife out of the church, she's still beautiful to other men, and jealousy is a terrible thing."

An uneasiness entered Vachon's eyes.

"In fact, I've wondered what's at the core of that emotion for men, and I think that jealousy goes back to something very basic."

I paused, considering for a moment whether Vachon would ever love any woman enough to be jealous.

"And what is the reason for men's jealousy?" Vachon was trying for a casual, amused tone, but his voice had moved up half an octave.

"Over the centuries, before the scientists and their laboratories, how many men looked into their children's faces, searching for any resemblance, wanting to ask: 'Are you mine?'"

I now had Vachon's full attention. He had forgotten about the fork that his right hand was still holding.

"Now, if a husband found out that his wife was having an affair, I wonder how he'd react," I said. "First, he might ask himself whose fault it was. Who was the pursuer — the wife or the lover? Or was the lover the kind of man for whom women were just a game? Could he make any woman feel beautiful and desired — make her feel as if she had found the perfect, romantic lover?

"Then, what would the husband do? Get angry? Get quiet? Want to talk it out? We'd all react a little differently, but some would decide to solve the problem — permanently. And, how they'd go about it would probably depend on what they knew.

"A carpenter, for example, would own a nail gun, and the next time he was pouring cement for a building's foundation, he'd have his problem solved. And a fisherman? Well, he'd probably take his wife's lover out for a boat trip, along with some rope, a rock, and a net." I paused. "But, a chef? I wonder what a chef would do?"

I looked at Vachon, who was now incapable of speech.

"I think that a chef would look into all his cookbooks and find all the foods that had warnings; then he would invite his wife's lover to share a meal." I looked at the bowl and plate in front of Vachon. "For example, maybe he makes the soup with an extra ingredient — the botulism bacillus; then he might serve Death Cap mushrooms with the white ridge

245

around their stems, and complete the menu with a Japanese delicacy — the poisonous fish 'fugu,' which is delicious, but will kill you if it's not gutted just right. And maybe a very angry husband would serve all three to his wife's lover, just to make sure the job was done right."

I smiled amiably at Vachon. "But, I don't have to worry about you, Jean-Louis, my good friend, my best man. You would never do anything like that — not with Carolyn. Now, as the chef who made this meal, I want you to know how much pleasure it gives me to watch you eat."

Vachon stared at me, frozen with fear.

"Eat up," I said, holding my smile. "Otherwise, Jean-Louis, I will start to wonder if there might be something between you and my wife. Go on."

Vachon dropped his eyes to my plate and saw that my fish, leeks and mushrooms, and soup were all untouched. The ratatouille was the only thing I'd eaten. He suddenly noticed the fork in his right hand, a piece of fish speared on its four tines. Vachon started to lift the fork to his mouth, but his hand only moved a few inches. The fork dropped to his plate.

"I'm not hungry," he said, his French accent suddenly thick.

"I understand," I said. "A man can suddenly lose his appetite; it happens. So, let us just sit here for a while and enjoy your good wine. It will help you digest your meal that much faster."

Vachon was a broken man. He stood up and smiled a

ghastly smile. "I must go," he said. "I just remembered an appointment." And the Frenchman shot out of the kitchen. I heard the heavy front door close.

The nearest hospital was Bellevue. I guessed that Vachon would be there in about 10 minutes. I've never had my stomach pumped, but I've heard it's a miserable experience. I looked down at the plate of food in front of me and realized that my appetite was back. I picked up a fork, cut a large piece of fish, and tasted it. Excellent. I've always enjoyed the puffer fish, a safe, distant cousin to the famous fugu.

The dining-room door swung open. I glanced up at the clock — 5 p.m. exactly. My wife is a wonderfully prompt woman.

"Edward! I just saw Jean-Louis jump into a taxi. He was screaming to be taken to a hospital. What happened?"

"He thinks that someone poisoned him," I said, and took a sip of wine.

"But who would do that?"

"I would," I said, "if I thought he was having an affair with my wife."

Awareness came into her eyes, and, I think, a bit of relief. Sometimes, the hardest part of a mistake is ending it. Carolyn looked at me for a long moment, then sat on the stool where my old friend had been. She looked down at the half-eaten meal.

"Do you have a plate for me?" she asked quietly.

I shook my head.

247

"I deserve it," she said.

"You probably do," I replied.

I raised my left hand, took off my gold wedding band, and put it on the metal counter between us, next to the bottle of Vachon wine. Carolyn stared down at the ring that, in three years, she'd never seen off my finger.

"Your choice," I said. "What will it be?"

Carolyn looked up at me, then down at the ring and the bottle of wine. Without hesitation, she picked up the Vachon, and my heart sank. So it hadn't been just an affair.

"There's no choice," she said, and turned away from me. With a flick of her wrist, she tossed the dark bottle 10 feet into the trash bin below the cutting board.

Carolyn turned back to me. "Do you have another bottle of wine that you could open? Something American — something that goes well with confession?"

I studied my wife's face, the face that I wanted to see every day for the rest of my life.

"I'm sure I do," I said. "Red or white?" ♦

AFTERWORD

——◆◆◆——

Before I began writing fiction, I wondered where writers got their ideas. After seventeen Row 22 stories, I can tell you the answer: from everywhere.

The stories that you've just read (and if you haven't read them, stop reading this because I'm going to give away some of the endings) demanded a variety of themes, characters, and storylines. If United's frequent fliers caught me plowing the same field over and over, they would stop reading the Row 22 series. For that reason, I was always looking for something new — not a gimmick, but an idea with an element of humanity.

The first hint of a tale can come from remarkably diverse circumstances. In 1998, I was hired to write a screenplay based upon "A Schedule to Keep." I went to England to do research and, while driving through the hills of North Yorkshire, I turned on the radio just in time to hear the BBC newsreader say: "... the return of the stolen paintings ..." and I immediately turned off the radio. I didn't want to get tethered to the reality surrounding those words. For the next four hours, I drove in silence, thinking about that half-sentence, and about my father, who had recently died, and a dishonest woman whom I had known. By the end of the day,

I had the foundation for "Trust Me."

"The Return of Raspel" came from the most ordinary of circumstances. I was doing some outdoor work and listening to a book-on-tape of a Robert Ludlum novel when I began to wonder what it would be like if Ludlum had suddenly met someone like one of his characters — or maybe the character himself — and there was a premise worth playing with.

Other stories took much longer to evolve. Long before the Row 22 series, I read a biography of the movie producer Samuel Goldwyn, who as a teenager left his home in Poland and walked across Europe in order to reach America. It took me a few years, but I finally figured out how to make that single, extraordinary act of determination fit into a Row 22 story. "My Father's Gift" elicited numerous e-mails from people who said that Józef Glodek's story was nearly identical to that of their immigrant ancestor. A century ago, tens of thousands of people made that walk across Europe, and I still find it awe-inspiring.

Other stories came from people whom I knew well — or not at all. During college in Baltimore, I went out with a girl whose parents were wonderful people. After graduation, although I stopped seeing her, whenever I went back to Baltimore, I would always visit her parents. When the mother began to fail physically, her husband responded with absolute devotion, he was not capable of anything different. He is as admirable as anyone I know, and he is the sole reason for "Photographs and Memories."

One summer afternoon on Cape Cod, I saw a boy of about nine years climbing up to the highest branches of a tree while his sister, about five years old and holding a stuffed bear, stood independently away from the tree, although worriedly watching her brother. As he climbed, he kept checking to see where his sister was. When he came down, he said that it was time to go home for dinner. Their house was on the other side of the road and, when the boy reached the road's edge, he stopped and looked at his sister, who was keeping her independent distance of 15 feet. "Lydia," he said with tangible concern, "you have to cross the road next to me." Head down, she replied, "Okay," and walked over to her brother. They crossed together, then she went back to her five-year-old's independent distance — and I understood that he was absolutely protective of her, and she was absolutely loyal to him. And that is the heart of "Brother and Sister."

A friend from my newspaper days now works as the spokesman at a Connecticut hospital. While giving me a tour, he told me about a young girl and the highly publicized story of her need for a liver transplant. The night that a liver match arrived, she was rushed into surgery, but she was too weak and had endured too much. Her body shut down in the first minutes of the operation. My friend was at home when he received the telephone call from the operating room. Before calling the local newspapers and television stations, he went out to his backyard, away from his house, so that his children would not hear his voice crack as he reported the death of a child their own age. My friend's life was nothing like Charlie Elliott's, but that moment was the basis for "Here Tomorrow."

Occasionally, a story will develop from a few words that bubble to the surface of one's imagination and will not go away. For several months, I kept thinking about the same simple, declarative statement: "I am an honest man. I do not lie to my friends; I do not lie to my enemies; I do not lie to myself." Finally, I found the right character to say those words, and then the right story. "A Promise to Eddie Gray" now starts with those 25 words, exactly as they first came to mind.

Finally, a few weeks after "A Schedule to Keep" appeared, I received a long letter from a woman in New Zealand. She had a question that was important to her. "The last line of your story ("Marry for love.") affected me so deeply," she wrote, "that I need to know something — do you really believe it, or were you just writing an entertaining story?" I wrote back and told her the truth, that I believed in the story's last line. Now, six years later, if she were to ask me again, I could add something else, I could add a simple truth: You write what you are. That, I've learned, is the real answer to the question, "Where do stories come from?"

— Frederick Waterman
July 17, 2003